This Graphyco edition is an annotated republication of *Fifty Famous Stories Retold and Other Tales* by James Baldwin.

In order to provide historical context, Graphyco has included a biographical introduction of the author. None of those parts may be reproduced in any form or by any means without permission from the publisher except in the case of brief quotations

CONTENT

KING ALFRED AND THE CAKES.	1
KING ALFRED AND THE BEGGAR.	3
KING CANUTE ON THE SEASHORE.	4
THE SONS OF WILLIAM THE CONQUEROR.	7
THE WHITE SHIP.	10
KING JOHN AND THE ABBOT.	12
I. THE THREE QUESTIONS.	12
II. THE THREE ANSWERS.	14
A STORY OF ROBIN HOOD.	16
BRUCE AND THE SPIDER.	21
THE BLACK DOUGLAS.	22
THREE MEN OF GOTHAM.	25
OTHER WISE MEN OF GOTHAM.	28
THE MILLER OF THE DEE.	31
SIR PHILIP SIDNEY.	33
THE UNGRATEFUL SOLDIER.	34
SIR HUMPHREY GILBERT.	36
SIR WALTER RALEIGH.	36
POCAHONTAS.	39
GEORGE WASHINGTON AND HIS HATCHET.	40
GRACE DARLING.	41
THE STORY OF WILLIAM TELL.	43
ARNOLD WINKELRIED.	45
THE BELL OF ATRI.	46
HOW NAPOLEON CROSSED THE ALPS.	51
THE STORY OF CINCINNATUS.	52
THE STORY OF REGULUS.	55
CORNELIA'S JEWELS.	57
ANDROCLUS AND THE LION.	59
HORATIUS AT THE BRIDGE.	62
JULIUS CÆSAR.	64
THE SWORD OF DAMOCLES.	65
DAMON AND PYTHIAS.	68
A LACONIC ANSWER.	70
THE UNGRATEFUL GUEST.	70
ALEXANDER AND BUCEPHALUS.	72
DIOGENES THE WISE MAN.	74

THE BRAVE THREE HUNDRED.	76
SOCRATES AND HIS HOUSE.	77
THE KING AND HIS HAWK.	77
DOCTOR GOLDSMITH.	81
THE KINGDOMS.	82
THE BARMECIDE FEAST.	84
THE ENDLESS TALE.	87
THE BLIND MEN AND THE ELEPHANT.	89
MAXIMILIAN AND THE GOOSE BOY.	90
THE INCHCAPE ROCK.	94
WHITTINGTON AND HIS CAT.	96
I. THE CITY.	96
II. THE KITCHEN.	98
III. THE VENTURE.	99
IV. THE CAT.	101
V. THE FORTUNE.	103
CASABIANCA.	106
ANTONIO CANOVA.	107
PICCIOLA.	111
MIGNON.	115
OTHER TALES	119
JUPITER AND HIS MIGHTY COMPANY.	119
THE GOLDEN AGE.	120
THE STORY OF PROMETHEUS.	123
THE FLOOD.	131
THE STORY OF IO.	135

ABOUT THE AUTHOR

James Baldwin (1841-1925) was born in Indiana, United States, and made a career as an administrator and educator in the state starting at the age of 24. He served as the superintendent of Indiana's school system for 18 years and then went on to become a widely published textbook editor and children's author in the subjects of mythology, biography, legends and others. He wrote over thirty books about famous people in history and retold classical stories. His publications numbered 54 volumes. It is estimated that 26 million copies of his works sold worldwide, including in China and Indonesia.

KING ALFRED AND THE CAKES.

Many years ago there lived in Eng-land a wise and good king whose name was Al-fred. No other man ever did so much for his country as he; and people now, all over the world, speak of him as Alfred the Great.

In those days a king did not have a very easy life. There was war almost all the time, and no one else could lead his army into battle so well as he. And so, between ruling and fighting, he had a busy time of it indeed.

A fierce, rude people, called the Danes, had come from over the sea, and were fighting the Eng-lish. There were so many of them, and they were so bold and strong, that for a long time they gained every battle. If they kept on, they would soon be the masters of the whole country.

At last, after a great battle, the English army was broken up and scattered. Every man had to save himself in the best way he could. King Alfred fled alone, in great haste, through the woods and swamps.

Late in the day the king came to the hut of a wood-cut-ter. He was very tired and hungry, and he begged the wood-cut-ter's wife to give him something to eat and a place to sleep in her hut.

The wom-an was baking some cakes upon the hearth, and she looked with pity upon the poor, ragged fellow who seemed so hungry. She had no thought that he was the king.

"Yes," she said, "I will give you some supper if you will watch these cakes. I want to go out and milk the cow; and you must see that they do not burn while I am gone."

King Alfred was very willing to watch the cakes, but he had far greater things to think about. How was he going to get his army to-geth-er again? And how was he going to drive the fierce Danes out of the land? He forgot his hunger; he forgot the cakes; he forgot that he was in the woodcutter's hut. His mind was busy making plans for to-mor-row.

In a little while the wom-an came back. The cakes were smoking on the hearth. They were burned to a crisp. Ah, how angry she was!

"You lazy fellow!" she cried. "See what you have done! You want some-thing to eat, but you do not want to work!"

I have been told that she even struck the king with a stick; but I can hardly be-lieve that she was so ill-na-tured.

The king must have laughed to himself at the thought of being scolded in this way; and he was so hungry that he did not mind the woman's angry words half so much as the loss of the cakes.

I do not know whether he had any-thing to eat that night, or whether he had to go to bed without his supper. But it was not many days until he had gath-ered his men to-geth-er again, and had beaten the Danes in a great battle.

KING ALFRED AND THE BEGGAR.

At one time the Danes drove King Alfred from his kingdom, and he had to lie hidden for a long time on a little is-land in a river.

One day, all who were on the is-land, except the king and queen and one servant, went out to fish. It was a very lonely place, and no one could get to it except by a boat. About noon a ragged beggar came to the king's door, and asked for food.

The king called the servant, and asked, "How much food have we in the house?"

"My lord," said the servant, "we have only one loaf and a little wine."

Then the king gave thanks to God, and said, "Give half of the loaf and half of the wine to this poor man."

The servant did as he was bidden. The beggar thanked the king for his kindness, and went on his way.

In the after-noon the men who had gone out to fish came back. They had three boats full of fish, and they said, "We have caught more fish to-day than in all the other days that we have been on this island."

The king was glad, and he and his people were more hopeful than they had ever been before.

When night came, the king lay awake for a long time, and thought about the things that had happened that day. At last he fancied that he saw a great light like the sun; and in the midst of the light there stood an old man with black hair, holding an open book in his hand.

It may all have been a dream, and yet to the king it seemed very real indeed. He looked and wondered, but was not afraid.

"Who are you?" he asked of the old man.

"Alfred, my son, be brave," said the man; "for I am the one to whom you gave this day the half of all the food that you had. Be strong and joyful of heart, and listen to what I say. Rise up early in the morning and blow your horn three times, so loudly that the Danes may hear it. By nine o'clock, five hundred men will be around you ready to be led into battle. Go forth bravely, and within seven days your en-e-mies shall be beaten, and you shall go back to your kingdom to reign in peace."

Then the light went out, and the man was seen no more.

In the morning the king arose early, and crossed over to the mainland. Then he blew his horn three times very loudly; and when his friends heard it they were glad, but the Danes were filled with fear.

At nine o'clock, five hundred of his bravest soldiers stood around him ready for battle. He spoke, and told them what he had seen and heard in his dream; and when he had fin-ished, they all cheered loudly, and said that they would follow him and fight for him so long as they had strength.

So they went out bravely to battle; and they beat the Danes, and drove them back into their own place. And King Alfred ruled wisely and well over all his people for the rest of his days.

KING CANUTE ON THE SEASHORE.

A hundred years or more after the time of Alfred the Great there was a king of England named Ca-nuté. King Canute was a Dane; but the Danes were not so fierce and cruel then as they had been when they were at war with King Alfred.

The great men and of-fi-cers who were around King Canute were always praising him.

"You are the greatest man that ever lived," one would say.

Then an-oth-er would say, "O king! there can never be an-oth-er man so mighty as you."

And another would say, "Great Canute, there is nothing in the world that dares to dis-o-bey you."

The king was a man of sense, and he grew very tired of hearing such foolish speeches.

One day he was by the sea-shore, and his of-fi-cers were with him. They were praising him, as they were in the habit of doing. He thought that now he would teach them a lesson, and so he bade them set his chair on the beach close by the edge of the water.

"Am I the greatest man in the world?" he asked.

"O king!" they cried, "there is no one so mighty as you."

"Do all things obey me?" he asked.

"There is nothing that dares to dis-o-bey you, O king!" they said. "The world bows before you, and gives you honor."

"Will the sea obey me?" he asked; and he looked down at the little waves which were lapping the sand at his feet.

"Sea, I command you to come no farther!"

The foolish officers were puzzled, but they did not dare to say "No."

"Command it, O king! and it will obey," said one.

"Sea," cried Canute, "I command you to come no farther! Waves, stop your rolling, and do not dare to touch my feet!"

But the tide came in, just as it always did. The water rose higher and higher. It came up around the king's chair, and wet not only his feet, but also his robe. His officers stood about him, alarmed, and won-der-ing whether he was not mad.

Then Canute took off his crown, and threw it down upon the sand.

"I shall never wear it again," he said. "And do you, my men, learn a lesson from what you have seen. There is only one King who is all-powerful; and it is he who rules the sea, and holds the ocean in the hollow of his hand. It is he whom you ought to praise and serve above all others."

THE SONS OF WILLIAM THE CONQUEROR.

There was once a great king of England who was called Wil-liam the Con-quer-or, and he had three sons.

One day King Wil-liam seemed to be thinking of something that made him feel very sad; and the wise men who were about him asked him what was the matter.

"I am thinking," he said, "of what my sons may do after I am dead. For, unless they are wise and strong, they cannot keep the kingdom which I have won for them. Indeed, I am at a loss to know which one of the three ought to be the king when I am gone."

"O king!" said the wise men, "if we only knew what things your sons admire the most, we might then be able to tell what kind of men they will be. Perhaps, by asking each one of them a few ques-tions, we can find out which one of them will be best fitted to rule in your place."

"The plan is well worth trying, at least," said the king. "Have the boys come before you, and then ask them what you please."

The wise men talked with one another for a little while, and then agreed that the young princes should be brought in, one at a time, and that the same ques-tions should be put to each.

The first who came into the room was Robert. He was a tall, willful lad, and was nick-named Short Stocking.

"Fair sir," said one of the men, "answer me this question: If, instead of being a boy, it had pleased God that you should be a bird, what kind of a bird would you rather be?"

"A hawk," answered Robert. "I would rather be a hawk, for no other bird reminds one so much of a bold and gallant knight."

The next who came was young William, his father's name-sake and pet. His face was jolly and round, and because he had red hair he was nicknamed Rufus, or the Red.

"Fair sir," said the wise man, "answer me this question: If, instead of being a boy, it had pleased God that you should be a bird, what kind of a bird would you rather be?"

"An eagle," answered William. "I would rather be an eagle, because it is strong and brave. It is feared by all other birds, and is there-fore the king of them all."

Lastly came the youngest brother, Henry, with quiet steps and a sober, thought-ful look. He had been taught to read and write, and for that reason he was nick-named Beau-clerc, or the Hand-some Schol-ar.

"Fair sir," said the wise man, "answer me this question: If, instead of being a boy, it had pleased God that you should be a bird, what kind of a bird would you rather be?"

"A star-ling," said Henry. "I would rather be a star-ling, because it is good-mannered and kind and a joy to every one who sees it, and it never tries to rob or abuse its neigh-bor."

Then the wise men talked with one another for a little while, and when they had agreed among themselves, they spoke to the king.

"We find," said they, "that your eldest son, Robert, will be bold and gallant. He will do some great deeds, and make a name for himself; but in the end he will be over-come by his foes, and will die in prison.

"The second son, William, will be as brave and strong as the eagle; but he will be feared and hated for his cruel deeds. He will lead a wicked life, and will die a shameful death.

"The youngest son, Henry, will be wise and prudent and peaceful. He will go to war only when he is forced to do so by his enemies. He will be loved at home, and re-spect-ed abroad; and he will die in peace after having gained great pos-ses-sions."

Years passed by, and the three boys had grown up to be men. King William lay upon his death-bed, and again he thought of what would become of his sons when he was gone. Then he re-mem-bered what the wise men had told him; and so he de-clared that Robert should have the lands which he held in France, that William should be the King of England, and that Henry should have no land at all, but only a chest of gold.

So it hap-pened in the end very much as the wise men had fore-told. Robert, the Short Stocking, was bold and reckless, like the hawk which he so much admired. He lost all the lands that his father had left him, and was at last shut up in prison, where he was kept until he died.

William Rufus was so over-bear-ing and cruel that he was feared and hated by all his people. He led a wicked life, and was killed by one of his own men while hunting in the forest.

And Henry, the Handsome Scholar, had not only the chest of gold for his own, but he became by and by the King of England and the ruler of all the lands that his father had had in France.

THE WHITE SHIP.

King Henry, the Handsome Scholar, had one son, named William, whom he dearly loved. The young man was noble and brave, and every-body hoped that he would some day be the King of England.

One summer Prince William went with his father across the sea to look after their lands in France. They were wel-comed with joy by all their people there, and the young prince was so gallant and kind, that he won the love of all who saw him.

But at last the time came for them to go back to England. The king, with his wise men and brave knights, set sail early in the day; but Prince William with his younger friends waited a little while. They had had so joyous a time in France that they were in no great haste to tear them-selves away.

Then they went on board of the ship which was waiting to carry them home. It was a beau-ti-ful ship with white sails and white masts, and it had been fitted up on purpose for this voyage.

The sea was smooth, the winds were fair, and no one thought of danger. On the ship, every-thing had been ar-ranged to make the trip a pleasant one. There was music and dancing, and everybody was merry and glad.

The sun had gone down before the white-winged vessel was fairly out of the bay. But what of that? The moon was at its full, and it would give light enough; and before the dawn of the morrow, the narrow sea would be crossed. And so the prince, and the young people who were with him, gave themselves up to mer-ri-ment and feasting and joy.

The ear-li-er hours of the night passed by; and then there was a cry of alarm on deck. A moment after-ward there was a great crash. The ship had struck upon a rock. The water rushed in. She was sinking. Ah, where now were those who had lately been so heart-free and glad?

Every heart was full of fear. No one knew what to do. A small boat was quickly launched, and the prince with a few of his bravest friends leaped into it. They pushed off just as the ship was be-gin-ning to settle beneath the waves. Would they be saved?

They had rowed hardly ten yards from the ship, when there was a cry from among those that were left behind.

"Row back!" cried the prince. "It is my little sister. She must be saved!"

The men did not dare to disobey. The boat was again brought along-side of the sinking vessel. The prince stood up, and held out his arms for his sister. At that moment the ship gave a great lurch forward into the waves. One shriek of terror was heard, and then all was still save the sound of the moaning waters.

Ship and boat, prince and prin-cess, and all the gay com-pa-ny that had set sail from France, went down to the bottom together. One man clung to a floating plank, and was saved the next day. He was the only person left alive to tell the sad story.

When King Henry heard of the death of his son his grief was more than he could bear. His heart was broken. He had no more joy in life; and men say that no one ever saw him smile again.

Here is a poem about him that your teacher may read to you, and perhaps, after a while, you may learn it by heart.

HE NEVER SMILED AGAIN.

The bark that held the prince went down,The sweeping waves rolled on;And what was England's glorious crownTo him that wept a son?He lived, for life may long be borneEre sorrow breaks its chain:Why comes not death to those who mourn?He never smiled again.

There stood proud forms before his throne,The stately and the brave;But who could fill the place of one,—That one beneath the wave?Before him passed the young and fair,In pleasure's reckless train;But seas dashed o'er his son's bright hair—He never smiled again.

He sat where festal bowls went round;He heard the minstrel sing;He saw the tour-ney's victor crownedAmid the knightly ring. A murmur of the restless deepWas blent with every strain,A voice of winds that would not sleep—He never smiled again.

Hearts, in that time, closed o'er the traceOf vows once fondly poured,And strangers took the kins-man's placeAt many a joyous board;Graves which true love had bathed with tearsWere left to heaven's bright rain;Fresh hopes were born for other years—He never smiled again!

MRS.

KING JOHN AND THE ABBOT.

I. THE THREE QUESTIONS.

There was once a king of England whose name was John. He was a bad king; for he was harsh and cruel to his people, and so long as he could have his own way, he did not care what became of other folks. He was the worst king that England ever had.

Now, there was in the town of Can´ter-bur-y a rich old abbot who lived in grand style in a great house called the Abbey. Every day a hundred noble men sat down with him to dine; and fifty brave knights, in fine velvet coats and gold chains, waited upon him at his table.

When King John heard of the way in which the abbot lived, he made up his mind to put a stop to it. So he sent for the old man to come and see him.

"How now, my good abbot?" he said. "I hear that you keep a far better house than I. How dare you do such a thing? Don't you know that no man in the land ought to live better than the king? And I tell you that no man shall."

"O king!" said the abbot, "I beg to say that I am spending nothing but what is my own. I hope that you will not think ill of me for making things pleasant for my friends and the brave knights who are with me."

"Think ill of you?" said the king. "How can I help but think ill of you? All that there is in this broad land is mine by right; and how do you dare to put me to shame by living in grander style than I? One would think that you were trying to be king in my place."

"Oh, do not say so!" said the abbot "For I"—

"Not another word!" cried the king. "Your fault is plain, and unless you can answer me three questions, your head shall be cut off, and all your riches shall be mine."

"I will try to answer them, O king!" said the abbot.

"Well, then," said King John, "as I sit here with my crown of gold on my head, you must tell me to within a day just how long I shall live. Sec-ond-ly, you must tell me how soon I shall ride round the whole world; and lastly, you shall tell me what I think."

"O king!" said the abbot, "these are deep, hard questions, and I cannot answer them just now. But if you will give me two weeks to think about them, I will do the best that I can."

"Two weeks you shall have," said the king; "but if then you fail to answer me, you shall lose your head, and all your lands shall be mine."

The abbot went away very sad and in great fear. He first rode to Oxford. Here was a great school, called a u-ni-ver′si-ty, and he wanted to see if any of the wise pro-fess-ors could help him. But they shook their heads, and said that there was nothing about King John in any of their books.

Then the abbot rode down to Cam-bridge, where there was another u-ni-ver-si-ty. But not one of the teachers in that great school could help him.

At last, sad and sor-row-ful, he rode toward home to bid his friends and his brave knights good-by. For now he had not a week to live.

II. THE THREE ANSWERS.

As the abbot was riding up the lane which led to his grand house, he met his shep-herd going to the fields.

"Welcome home, good master!" cried the shepherd. "What news do you bring us from great King John?"

"Sad news, sad news," said the abbot; and then he told him all that had happened.

"Cheer up, cheer up, good master," said the shepherd. "Have you never yet heard that a fool may teach a wise man wit? I think I can help you out of your trouble."

"You help me!" cried the abbot "How? how?"

"Well," answered the shepherd, "you know that everybody says that I look just like you, and that I have some-times been mis-tak-en for you. So, lend me your servants and your horse and your gown, and I will go up to London and see the king. If nothing else can be done, I can at least die in your place."

"My good shepherd," said the abbot, "you are very, very kind; and I have a mind to let you try your plan. But if the worst comes to the worst, you shall not die for me. I will die for myself."

So the shepherd got ready to go at once. He dressed himself with great care. Over his shepherd's coat he threw the abbot's long gown, and he bor-rowed the abbot's cap and golden staff. When all was ready, no one in the world would have thought that he was not the great man himself. Then he mounted his horse, and with a great train of servants set out for London.

Of course the king did not know him.

"Welcome, Sir Abbot!" he said. "It is a good thing that you have come back. But, prompt as you are, if you fail to answer my three questions, you shall lose your head."

"I am ready to answer them, O king!" said the shepherd.

"Indeed, indeed!" said the king, and he laughed to himself. "Well, then, answer my first question: How long shall I live? Come, you must tell me to the very day."

"You shall live," said the shepherd, "until the day that you die, and not one day longer. And you shall die when you take your last breath, and not one moment before."

"You shall live until the day that you die."

The king laughed.

"You are witty, I see," he said. "But we will let that pass, and say that your answer is right. And now tell me how soon I may ride round the world."

"You must rise with the sun," said the shepherd, "and you must ride with the sun until it rises again the next morning. As soon as you do that, you will find that you have ridden round the world in twenty-four hours."

The king laughed again. "Indeed," he said, "I did not think that it could be done so soon. You are not only witty, but you are wise, and we will let this answer pass. And now comes my third and last question: What do I think?"

"That is an easy question," said the shepherd. "You think that I am the Abbot of Can-ter-bur-y. But, to tell you the truth, I am only his poor shepherd, and I have come to beg your pardon for him and for me." And with that, he threw off his long gown.

The king laughed loud and long.

"A merry fellow you are," said he, "and you shall be the Abbot of Canterbury in your master's place."

"O king! that cannot be," said the shepherd; "for I can neither read nor write."

"Very well, then," said the king, "I will give you something else to pay you for this merry joke. I will give you four pieces of silver every week as long as you live. And when you get home, you may tell the old abbot that you have brought him a free pardon from King John."

A STORY OF ROBIN HOOD.

In the rude days of King Rich-ard and King John there were many great woods in England. The most famous of these was Sher-wood forest, where the king often went to hunt deer. In this forest there lived a band of daring men called out-laws.

They had done something that was against the laws of the land, and had been forced to hide themselves in the woods to save their lives. There they spent their time in roaming about among the trees, in hunting the king's deer, and in robbing rich trav-el-ers that came that way.

There were nearly a hundred of these outlaws, and their leader was a bold fellow called Robin Hood. They were dressed in suits of green, and armed with bows and arrows; and sometimes they carried long wooden lances and broad-swords, which they knew how to handle well. When-ever they had taken anything, it was brought and laid at the feet of Robin Hood, whom they called their king. He then di-vid-ed it fairly among them, giving to each man his just share.

Robin never allowed his men to harm any-body but the rich men who lived in great houses and did no work. He was always kind to the poor, and he often sent help to them; and for that reason the common people looked upon him as their friend.

Long after he was dead, men liked to talk about his deeds. Some praised him, and some blamed him. He was, indeed, a rude, lawless fellow; but at that time, people did not think of right and wrong as they do now.

A great many songs were made up about Robin Hood, and these songs were sung in the cot-ta-ges and huts all over the land for hundreds of years after-ward.

Here is a little story that is told in one of those songs:—

Robin Hood was standing one day under a green tree by the road-side. While he was lis-ten-ing to the birds among the leaves, he saw a young man passing by. This young man was dressed in a fine suit of bright red cloth; and, as he tripped gayly along the road, he seemed to be as happy as the day.

"I will not trou-ble him," said Robin Hood, "for I think he is on his way to his wedding."

The next day Robin stood in the same place. He had not been there long when he saw the same young man coming down the road. But he did not seem to be so happy this time. He had left his scarlet coat at home, and at every step he sighed and groaned.

"Ah the sad day! the sad day!" he kept saying to himself.

Then Robin Hood stepped out from under the tree, and said,—

"I say, young man! Have you any money to spare for my merry men and me?"

"I have nothing at all," said the young man, "but five shil-lings and a ring."

"A gold ring?" asked Robin.

"Yes?" said the young man, "it is a gold ring. Here it is."

"Ah, I see!" said Robin: "it is a wedding ring."

"I have kept it these seven years," said the young man; "I have kept it to give to my bride on our wedding day. We were going to be married yes-ter-day. But her father has prom-ised her to a rich old man whom she never saw. And now my heart is broken."

"What is your name?" asked Robin.

"My name is Allin-a-Dale," said the young man.

"What will you give me, in gold or fee," said Robin, "if I will help you win your bride again in spite of the rich old man to whom she has been promised?"

"I have no money," said Allin, "but I will promise to be your servant."

"How many miles is it to the place where the maiden lives?" asked Robin.

"It is not far," said Allin. "But she is to be married this very day, and the church is five miles away."

Then Robin made haste to dress himself as a harper; and in the afternoon he stood in the door of the church.

"Who are you?" said the bishop, "and what are you doing here?"

"I am a bold harper," said Robin, "the best in the north country."

"I am glad you have come," said the bishop kindly. "There is no music that I like so well as that of the harp. Come in, and play for us."

"I will go in," said Robin Hood; "but I will not give you any music until I see the bride and bridegroom."

Just then an old man came in. He was dressed in rich clothing, but was bent with age, and was feeble and gray. By his side walked a fair young girl. Her cheeks were very pale, and her eyes were full of tears.

"This is no match," said Robin. "Let the bride choose for herself."

Then he put his horn to his lips, and blew three times. The very next minute, four and twenty men, all dressed in green, and car-ry-ing long bows in their hands, came running across the fields. And as they marched into the church, all in a row, the fore-most among them was Allin-a-Dale.

"Now whom do you choose?" said Robin to the maiden.

"I choose Allin-a-Dale," she said, blushing.

"And Allin-a-Dale you shall have," said Robin; "and he that takes you from Allin-a-Dale shall find that he has Robin Hood to deal with."

And so the fair maiden and Allin-a-Dale were married then and there, and the rich old man went home in a great rage.

"And thus having ended this merry wedding,The bride looked like a queen:And so they re-turned to the merry green wood,Amongst the leaves so green."

BRUCE AND THE SPIDER.

There was once a king of Scot-land whose name was Robert Bruce. He had need to be both brave and wise, for the times in which he lived were wild and rude. The King of England was at war with him, and had led a great army into Scotland to drive him out of the land.

Battle after battle had been fought. Six times had Bruce led his brave little army against his foes; and six times had his men been beaten, and driven into flight. At last his army was scat-tered, and he was forced to hide himself in the woods and in lonely places among the moun-tains.

One rainy day, Bruce lay on the ground under a rude shed, lis-ten-ing to the patter of the drops on the roof above him. He was tired and sick at heart, and ready to give up all hope. It seemed to him that there was no use for him to try to do anything more.

As he lay thinking, he saw a spider over his head, making ready to weave her web. He watched her as she toiled slowly and with great care. Six times she tried to throw her frail thread from one beam to another, and six times it fell short.

"Poor thing!" said Bruce: "you, too, know what it is to fail."

But the spider did not lose hope with the sixth failure. With still more care, she made ready to try for the seventh time. Bruce almost forgot his own troubles as he watched her swing herself out upon the slender line. Would she fail again? No! The thread was carried safely to the beam, and fas-tened there.

"I, too, will try a seventh time!" cried Bruce.

He arose and called his men together. He told them of his plans, and sent them out with mes-sa-ges of cheer to his dis-heart-ened people. Soon there was an army of brave Scotch-men around him. Another battle was fought, and the King of England was glad to go back into his own country.

I have heard it said, that, after that day, no one by the name of Bruce would ever hurt a spider. The lesson which the little crea-ture had taught the king was never for-got-ten.

THE BLACK DOUGLAS.

In Scotland, in the time of King Robert Bruce, there lived a brave man whose name was Doug-las. His hair and beard were black and long, and his face was tanned and dark; and for this reason people nicknamed him the Black Douglas. He was a good friend of the king, and one of his strongest helpers.

In the war with the English, who were trying to drive Bruce from Scotland, the Black Douglas did many brave deeds; and the English people became very much afraid of him. By and by the fear of him spread all through the land. Nothing could frighten an English lad more than to tell him that the Black Douglas was not far away. Women would tell their chil-dren, when they were naughty, that the Black Douglas would get them; and this would make them very quiet and good.

There was a large cas-tle in Scotland which the English had taken early in the war. The Scot-tish soldiers wanted very much to take it again, and the Black Douglas and his men went one day to see what they could do. It happened to be a hol-i-day, and most of the English soldiers in the cas-tle were eating and drinking and having a merry time. But they had left watch-men on the wall to see that the Scottish soldiers did not come upon them un-a-wares; and so they felt quite safe.

In the e-ven-ing, when it was growing dark, the wife of one of the soldiers went up on the wall with her child in her arms. As she looked over into the fields below the castle, she saw some dark objects moving toward the foot of the wall. In the dusk she could not make out what they were, and so she pointed them out to one of the watch-men.

"Pooh, pooh!" said the watchman. "Those are nothing to frighten us. They are the farmer's cattle, trying to find their way home. The farmer himself is en-joy-ing the hol-i-day, and he has forgotten to bring them in. If the Douglas should happen this way before morning, he will be sorry for his care-less-ness."

But the dark objects were not cattle. They were the Black Douglas and his men, creeping on hands and feet toward the foot of the castle wall. Some of them were dragging ladders behind them through the grass. They would soon be climbing to the top of the wall. None of the English soldiers dreamed that they were within many miles of the place.

The woman watched them until the last one had passed around a corner out of sight. She was not afraid, for in the dark-en-ing twi-light they looked indeed like cattle. After a little while she began to sing to her child:—

"Hush ye, hush ye, little pet ye,Hush ye, hush ye, do not fret ye,The Black Douglas shall not get ye."

"Don't be so sure about that!"

All at once a gruff voice was heard behind her, saying, "Don't be so sure about that!"

She looked around, and there stood the Black Douglas himself. At the same moment a Scottish soldier climbed off a ladder and leaped upon the wall; and then there came another and another and another, until the wall was covered with them. Soon there was hot fighting in every part of the castle. But the English were so taken by surprise that they could not do much. Many of them were killed, and in a little while the Black Douglas and his men were the masters of the castle, which by right be-longed to them.

As for the woman and her child, the Black Douglas would not suffer any one to harm them. After a while they went back to England; and whether the mother made up any more songs about the Black Douglas I cannot tell.

THREE MEN OF GOTHAM.

There is a town in England called Go-tham, and many merry stories are told of the queer people who used to live there.

One day two men of Go-tham met on a bridge. Hodge was coming from the market, and Peter was going to the market.

"Where are you going?" said Hodge.

"I am going to the market to buy sheep," said Peter.

"Buy sheep?" said Hodge. "And which way will you bring them home?"

"I shall bring them over this bridge," said Peter.

"No, you shall not," said Hodge.

"Yes, but I will," said Peter.

"You shall not," said Hodge.

"I will," said Peter.

Then they beat with their sticks on the ground as though there had been a hundred sheep between them.

"Take care!" cried Peter. "Look out that my sheep don't jump on the bridge."

"I care not where they jump," said Hodge; "but they shall not go over it."

"But they shall," said Peter.

"Have a care," said Hodge; "for if you say too much, I will put my fingers in your mouth."

"Will you?" said Peter.

Just then another man of Gotham came from the market with a sack of meal on his horse. He heard his neigh-bors quar-rel-ing about sheep; but he could see no sheep between them, and so he stopped and spoke to them.

"Ah, you foolish fellows!" he cried. "It is strange that you will never learn wisdom.—Come here, Peter, and help me lay my sack on my shoul-der."

Peter did so, and the man carried his meal to the side of the bridge.

"Now look at me," he said, "and learn a lesson." And he opened the mouth of the sack, and poured all the meal into the river.

"Now, neighbors," he said, "can you tell how much meal is in my sack?"

"How much meal is in my sack?"

"There is none at all!" cried Hodge and Peter together.

"You are right," said the man; "and you that stand here and quarrel about nothing, have no more sense in your heads than I have meal in my sack!"

OTHER WISE MEN OF GOTHAM.

One day, news was brought to Gotham that the king was coming that way, and that he would pass through the town. This did not please the men of Gotham at all. They hated the king, for they knew that he was a cruel, bad man. If he came to their town, they would have to find food and lodg-ing for him and his men; and if he saw anything that pleased him, he would be sure to take it for his own. What should they do?

They met together to talk the matter over.

"Let us chop down the big trees in the woods, so that they will block up all the roads that lead into the town," said one of the wise men.

"Good!" said all the rest.

So they went out with their axes, and soon all the roads and paths to the town were filled with logs and brush. The king's horse-men would have a hard time of it getting into Gotham. They would either have to make a new road, or give up the plan al-to-geth-er, and go on to some other place.

When the king came, and saw that the road had been blocked up, he was very angry.

"Who chopped those trees down in my way?" he asked of two country lads that were passing by.

"The men of Gotham," said the lads.

"Well," said the king, "go and tell the men of Gotham that I shall send my sher-iff into their town, and have all their noses cut off."

The two lads ran to the town as fast as they could, and made known what the king had said.

Every-body was in great fright. The men ran from house to house, carrying the news, and asking one another what they should do.

"Our wits have kept the king out of the town," said one; "and so now our wits must save our noses."

"True, true!" said the others. "But what shall we do?"

Then one, whose name was Dobbin, and who was thought to be the wisest of them all, said, "Let me tell you something. Many a man has been punished because he was wise, but I have never heard of any one being harmed because he was a fool. So, when the king's sher-iff comes, let us all act like fools."

"Good, good!" cried the others. "We will all act like fools."

It was no easy thing for the king's men to open the roads; and while they were doing it, the king grew tired of waiting, and went back to London. But very early one morning, the sheriff with a party of fierce soldiers rode through the woods, and between the fields, toward Gotham. Just before they reached the town, they saw a queer sight. The old men were rolling big stones up the hill, and all the young men were looking on, and grunting very loudly.

The sheriff stopped his horses, and asked what they were doing.

"We are rolling stones up-hill to make the sun rise," said one of the old men.

"You foolish fellow!" said the sheriff. "Don't you know that the sun will rise without any help?"

"Ah! will it?" said the old man. "Well, I never thought of that. How wise you are!"

"And what are *you* doing?" said the sheriff to the young men.

"Oh, we do the grunting while our fathers do the working," they answered.

"I see," said the sheriff. "Well, that is the way the world goes every-where." And he rode on toward the town.

He soon came to a field where a number of men were building a stone wall.

"What are you doing?" he asked.

"Why, master," they answered, "there is a cuck-oo in this field, and we are building a wall around it so as to keep the bird from straying away."

"You foolish fellows!" said the sheriff. "Don't you know that the bird will fly over the top of your wall, no matter how high you build it?"

"Why, no," they said. "We never thought of that. How very wise you are!"

The sheriff next met a man who was carrying a door on his back.

"What are you doing?" he asked.

"I have just started on a long jour-ney," said the man.

"But why do you carry that door?" asked the sheriff.

"I left my money at home."

"Then why didn't you leave the door at home too?"

"I was afraid of thieves; and you see, if I have the door with me, they can't break it open and get in."

"You foolish fellow!" said the sheriff. "It would be safer to leave the door at home, and carry the money with you."

"Ah, would it, though?" said the man. "Now, I never thought of that. You are the wisest man that I ever saw."

Then the sheriff rode on with his men; but every one that they met was doing some silly thing.

"Truly I believe that the people of Gotham are all fools," said one of the horsemen.

"That is true," said another. "It would be a shame to harm such simple people."

"Let us ride back to London, and tell the king all about them," said the sheriff.

"Yes, let us do so," said the horsemen.

So they went back, and told the king that Gotham was a town of fools; and the king laughed, and said that if that was the case, he would not harm them, but would let them keep their noses.

THE MILLER OF THE DEE.

Once upon a time there lived on the banks of the River Dee a miller, who was the hap-pi-est man in England. He was always busy from morning till night, and he was always singing as merrily as any lark. He was so cheerful that he made everybody else cheerful; and people all over the land liked to talk about his pleasant ways. At last the king heard about him.

"I will go down and talk with this won-der-ful miller," he said. "Perhaps he can tell me how to be happy."

As soon as he stepped inside of the mill, he heard the miller singing:—

"I envy no-body—no, not I!—For I am as happy as I can be;And nobody envies me."

"You're wrong, my friend," said the king. "You're wrong as wrong can be. I envy you; and I would gladly change places with you, if I could only be as light-hearted as you are."

The miller smiled, and bowed to the king.

"I am sure I could not think of changing places with you, sir," he said.

"Now tell me," said the king, "what makes you so cheerful and glad here in your dusty mill, while I, who am king, am sad and in trouble every day."

The miller smiled again, and said, "I do not know why you are sad, but I can eas-i-ly tell why I am glad. I earn my own bread; I love my wife and my children; I love my friends, and they love me; and I owe not a penny to any man. Why should I not be happy? For here is the River Dee, and every day it turns my mill; and the mill grinds the corn that feeds my wife, my babes, and me."

"Say no more," said the king. "Stay where you are, and be happy still. But I envy you. Your dusty cap is worth more than my golden crown. Your mill does more for you than my kingdom can do for me. If there were more such men as you, what a good place this world would be! Good-by, my friend!"

The king turned about, and walked sadly away; and the miller went back to his work singing:—

"Oh, I'm as happy as happy can be,For I live by the side of the River Dee!"

SIR PHILIP SIDNEY.

A cruel battle was being fought. The ground was covered with dead and dying men. The air was hot and stifling. The sun shone down without pity on the wounded soldiers lying in the blood and dust.

One of these soldiers was a no-ble-man, whom everybody loved for his gen-tle-ness and kindness. Yet now he was no better off than the poorest man in the field. He had been wounded, and would die; and he was suf-fer-ing much with pain and thirst.

When the battle was over, his friends hurried to his aid. A soldier came running with a cup in his hand.

"Here, Sir Philip," he said, "I have brought you some clear, cool water from the brook. I will raise your head so that you can drink."

The cup was placed to Sir Philip's lips. How thank-ful-ly he looked at the man who had brought it! Then his eyes met those of a dying soldier who was lying on the ground close by. The wist-ful look in the poor man's face spoke plainer than words.

"Give the water to that man," said Sir Philip quickly; and then, pushing the cup toward him, he said, "Here, my comrade, take this. Thy need is greater than mine."

What a brave, noble man he was! The name of Sir Philip Sidney will never be for-got-ten; for it was the name of a Chris-tian gen-tle-man who always had the good of others in his mind. Was it any wonder that everybody wept when it was heard that he was dead?

It is said, that, on the day when he was carried to the grave, every eye in the land was filled with tears. Rich and poor, high and low, all felt that they had lost a friend; all mourned the death of the kindest, gentlest man that they had ever known.

THE UNGRATEFUL SOLDIER.

Here is another story of the bat-tle-field, and it is much like the one which I have just told you.

Not quite a hundred years after the time of Sir Philip Sidney there was a war between the Swedes and the Danes. One day a great battle was fought, and the Swedes were beaten, and driven from the field. A soldier of the Danes who had been slightly wounded was sitting on the ground. He was about to take a drink from a flask. All at once he heard some one say,—

"O sir! give me a drink, for I am dying."

It was a wounded Swede who spoke. He was lying on the ground only a little way off. The Dane went to him at once. He knelt down by the side of his fallen foe, and pressed the flask to his lips.

"Drink," said he, "for thy need is greater than mine."

Hardly had he spoken these words, when the Swede raised himself on his elbow. He pulled a pistol from his pocket, and shot at the man who would have be-friend-ed him. The bullet grazed the Dane's shoulder, but did not do him much harm.

"Ah, you rascal!" he cried. "I was going to befriend you, and you repay me by trying to kill me. Now I will punish you. I would have given you all the water, but now you shall have only half." And with that he drank the half of it, and then gave the rest to the Swede.

When the King of the Danes heard about this, he sent for the soldier and had him tell the story just as it was.

"Why did you spare the life of the Swede after he had tried to kill you?" asked the king.

"Because, sir," said the soldier, "I could never kill a wounded enemy."

"Then you deserve to be a no-ble-man," said the king. And he re-ward-ed him by making him a knight, and giving him a noble title.

SIR HUMPHREY GILBERT.

More than three hundred years ago there lived in England a brave man whose name was Sir Humphrey Gil-bert. At that time there were no white people in this country of ours. The land was covered with forests; and where there are now great cities and fine farms there were only trees and swamps among which roamed wild In-di-ans and wild beasts.

Sir Hum-phrey Gilbert was one of the first men who tried to make a set-tle-ment in A-mer-i-ca. Twice did he bring men and ships over the sea, and twice did he fail, and sail back for England. The second time, he was on a little ship called the "Squirrel." Another ship, called the "Golden Hind," was not far away. When they were three days from land, the wind failed, and the ships lay floating on the waves. Then at night the air grew very cold. A breeze sprang up from the east. Great white ice-bergs came drifting around them. In the morning the little ships were almost lost among the floating mountains of ice. The men on the "Hind" saw Sir Humphrey sitting on the deck of the "Squirrel" with an open book in his hand. He called to them and said,—

"Be brave, my friends! We are as near heaven on the sea as on the land."

Night came again. It was a stormy night, with mist and rain. All at once the men on the "Hind" saw the lights on board of the "Squirrel" go out. The little vessel, with brave Sir Humphrey and all his brave men, was swal-lowed up by the waves.

SIR WALTER RALEIGH.

There once lived in England a brave and noble man whose name was Walter Ra-leigh. He was not only brave and noble, but he was also handsome and polite; and for that reason the queen made him a knight, and called him Sir Walter Ra-leigh.

I will tell you about it.

When Raleigh was a young man, he was one day walking along a street in London. At that time the streets were not paved, and there were no side walks. Raleigh was dressed in very fine style, and he wore a beau-ti-ful scar-let cloak thrown over his shoulders.

As he passed along, he found it hard work to keep from stepping in the mud, and soiling his hand-some new shoes. Soon he came to a puddle of muddy water which reached from one side of the street to the other. He could not step across. Perhaps he could jump over it.

As he was thinking what he should do, he happened to look up. Who was it coming down the street, on the other side of the puddle?

It was E-liz-a-beth, the Queen of England, with her train of gen-tle-wom-en and waiting maids. She saw the dirty puddle in the street. She saw the handsome young man with the scar-let cloak, stand-ing by the side of it. How was she to get across?

Young Raleigh, when he saw who was coming, forgot about himself. He thought only of helping the queen. There was only one thing that he could do, and no other man would have thought of that.

He took off his scarlet cloak, and spread it across the puddle. The queen could step on it now, as on a beautiful carpet.

She walked across. She was safely over the ugly puddle, and her feet had not touched the mud. She paused a moment, and thanked the young man.

As she walked onward with her train, she asked one of the gen-tle-wom-en, "Who is that brave gen-tle-man who helped us so handsomely?"

"His name is Walter Raleigh," said the gentle-woman.

"He shall have his reward," said the queen.

Not long after that, she sent for Raleigh to come to her pal-ace.

The young man went, but he had no scarlet cloak to wear. Then, while all the great men and fine ladies of England stood around, the queen made him a knight. And from that time he was known as Sir Walter Raleigh, the queen's favorite.

Sir Walter Raleigh and Sir Humphrey Gilbert about whom I have already told you, were half-broth-ers.

When Sir Humphrey made his first voy-age to America, Sir Walter was with him. After that, Sir Walter tried sev-er-al times to send men to this country to make a set-tle-ment.

But those whom he sent found only great forests, and wild beasts, and sav-age In-di-ans. Some of them went back to England; some of them died for want of food; and some of them were lost in the woods. At last Sir Walter gave up trying to get people to come to America.

But he found two things in this country which the people of England knew very little about. One was the po-ta-to, the other was to-bac-co.

If you should ever go to Ireland, you may be shown the place where Sir Walter planted the few po-ta-toes which he carried over from America. He told his friends how the Indians used them for food; and he proved that they would grow in the Old World as well as in the New.

Sir Walter had seen the Indians smoking the leaves of the to-bac-co plant. He thought that he would do the same, and he carried some of the leaves to England. Englishmen had never used tobacco before that time; and all who saw Sir Walter puff-ing away at a roll of leaves thought that it was a strange sight.

One day as he was sitting in his chair and smoking, his servant came into the room. The man saw the smoke curling over his master's head, and he thought that he was on fire.

He ran out for some water. He found a pail that was quite full. He hurried back, and threw the water into Sir Walter's face. Of course the fire was all put out.

After that a great many men learned to smoke. And now tobacco is used in all countries of the world. It would have been well if Sir Walter Raleigh had let it alone.

POCAHONTAS.

There was once a very brave man whose name was John Smith. He came to this country many years ago, when there were great woods everywhere, and many wild beasts and Indians. Many tales are told of his ad-ven-tures, some of them true and some of them untrue. The most famous of all these is the fol-low-ing:—

One day when Smith was in the woods, some Indians came upon him, and made him their pris-on-er. They led him to their king, and in a short time they made ready to put him to death.

A large stone was brought in, and Smith was made to lie down with his head on it. Then two tall Indians with big clubs in their hands came forward. The king and all his great men stood around to see. The Indians raised their clubs. In another moment they would fall on Smith's head.

But just then a little Indian girl rushed in. She was the daugh-ter of the king, and her name was Po-ca-hon´tas. She ran and threw herself between Smith and the up-lift-ed clubs. She clasped Smith's head with her arms. She laid her own head upon his.

"O father!" she cried, "spare this man's life. I am sure he has done you no harm, and we ought to be his friends."

The men with the clubs could not strike, for they did not want to hurt the child. The king at first did not know what to do. Then he spoke to some of his war-riors, and they lifted Smith from the ground. They untied the cords from his wrists and feet, and set him free.

The next day the king sent Smith home; and several Indians went with him to protect him from harm.

After that, as long as she lived, Po-ca-hon-tas was the friend of the white men, and she did a great many things to help them.

GEORGE WASHINGTON AND HIS HATCHET.

When George Wash-ing-ton was quite a little boy, his father gave him a hatchet. It was bright and new, and George took great delight in going about and chopping things with it.

He ran into the garden, and there he saw a tree which seemed to say to him, "Come and cut me down!"

George had often seen his father's men chop down the great trees in the forest, and he thought that it would be fine sport to see this tree fall with a crash to the ground. So he set to work with his little hatchet, and, as the tree was a very small one, it did not take long to lay it low.

Soon after that, his father came home.

"Who has been cutting my fine young cherry tree?" he cried. "It was the only tree of its kind in this country, and it cost me a great deal of money."

He was very angry when he came into the house.

"If I only knew who killed that cherry tree," he cried, "I would—yes, I would"—

"Father!" cried little George. "I will tell you the truth about it. I chopped the tree down with my hatchet."

His father forgot his anger.

"George," he said, and he took the little fellow in his arms, "George, I am glad that you told me about it. I would rather lose a dozen cherry trees than that you should tell one false-hood."

GRACE DARLING.

It was a dark Sep-tem-ber morning. There was a storm at sea. A ship had been driven on a low rock off the shores of the Farne Islands. It had been broken in two by the waves, and half of it had been washed away. The other half lay yet on the rock, and those of the crew who were still alive were cling-ing to it. But the waves were dashing over it, and in a little while it too would be carried to the bottom.

Could any one save the poor, half-drowned men who were there?

On one of the islands was a light-house; and there, all through that stormy night, Grace Darling had listened to the storm.

Grace was the daughter of the light-house keeper, and she had lived by the sea as long as she could re-mem-ber.

In the darkness of the night, above the noise of the winds and waves, she heard screams and wild cries. When day-light came, she could see the wreck, a mile away, with the angry waters all around it. She could see the men clinging to the masts.

"We must try to save them!" she cried. "Let us go out in the boat at once!"

"It is of no use, Grace," said her father. "We cannot reach them."

He was an old man, and he knew the force of the mighty waves.

"We cannot stay here and see them die," said Grace. "We must at least try to save them."

Her father could not say, "No."

In a few minutes they were ready. They set off in the heavy lighthouse boat. Grace pulled one oar, and her father the other, and they made straight toward the wreck. But it was hard rowing against such a sea, and it seemed as though they would never reach the place.

At last they were close to the rock, and now they were in greater danger than before. The fierce waves broke against the boat, and it would have been dashed in pieces, had it not been for the strength and skill of the brave girl.

But after many trials, Grace's father climbed upon the wreck, while Grace herself held the boat. Then one by one the worn-out crew were helped on board. It was all that the girl could do to keep the frail boat from being drifted away, or broken upon the sharp edges of the rock.

Then her father clam-bered back into his place. Strong hands grasped the oars, and by and by all were safe in the lighthouse. There Grace proved to be no less tender as a nurse than she had been brave as a sailor. She cared most kindly for the ship-wrecked men until the storm had died away and they were strong enough to go to their own homes.

All this happened a long time ago, but the name of Grace Darling will never be forgotten. She lies buried now in a little church-yard by the sea, not far from her old home. Every year many people go there to see her grave; and there a mon-u-ment has been placed in honor of the brave girl. It is not a large mon-u-ment, but it is one that speaks of the noble deed which made Grace Darling famous. It is a figure carved in stone of a woman lying at rest, with a boat's oar held fast in her right hand.

THE STORY OF WILLIAM TELL.

The people of Swit-zer-land were not always free and happy as they are to-day. Many years ago a proud tyrant, whose name was Gessler, ruled over them, and made their lot a bitter one indeed.

One day this tyrant set up a tall pole in the public square, and put his own cap on the top of it; and then he gave orders that every man who came into the town should bow down before it. But there was one man, named William Tell, who would not do this. He stood up straight with folded arms, and laughed at the swinging cap. He would not bow down to Gessler himself.

When Gessler heard of this, he was very angry. He was afraid that other men would disobey, and that soon the whole country would rebel against him. So he made up his mind to punish the bold man.

William Tell's home was among the mountains, and he was a famous hunter. No one in all the land could shoot with bow and arrow so well as he. Gessler knew this, and so he thought of a cruel plan to make the hunter's own skill bring him to grief. He ordered that Tell's little boy should be made to stand up in the public square with an apple on his head; and then he bade Tell shoot the apple with one of his arrows.

Tell begged the tyrant not to have him make this test of his skill. What if the boy should move? What if the bow-man's hand should tremble? What if the arrow should not carry true?

"Will you make me kill my boy?" he said.

"Say no more," said Gessler. "You must hit the apple with your one arrow. If you fail, my sol-diers shall kill the boy before your eyes."

Then, without another word, Tell fitted the arrow to his bow. He took aim, and let it fly. The boy stood firm and still. He was not afraid, for he had all faith in his father's skill.

The arrow whistled through the air. It struck the apple fairly in the center, and carried it away. The people who saw it shouted with joy.

As Tell was turning away from the place, an arrow which he had hidden under his coat dropped to the ground.

"Fellow!" cried Gessler, "what mean you with this second arrow?"

"Tyrant!" was Tell's proud answer, "this arrow was for your heart if I had hurt my child."

And there is an old story, that, not long after this, Tell did shoot the tyrant with one of his arrows; and thus he set his country free.

ARNOLD WINKELRIED.

A great army was marching into Swit-zer-land. If it should go much farther, there would be no driving it out again. The soldiers would burn the towns, they would rob the farmers of their grain and sheep, they would make slaves of the people.

The men of Switzerland knew all this. They knew that they must fight for their homes and their lives. And so they came from the mountains and valleys to try what they could do to save their land. Some came with bows and arrows, some with scythes and pitch-forks, and some with only sticks and clubs.

But their foes kept in line as they marched along the road. Every soldier was fully armed. As they moved and kept close together, nothing could be seen of them but their spears and shields and shining armor. What could the poor country people do against such foes as these?

"We must break their lines," cried their leader; "for we cannot harm them while they keep together."

The bowmen shot their arrows, but they glanced off from the soldiers' shields. Others tried clubs and stones, but with no better luck. The lines were still un-bro-ken. The soldiers moved stead-i-ly onward; their shields lapped over one another; their thousand spears looked like so many long bris-tles in the sun-light. What cared they for sticks and stones and hunts-men's arrows?

"If we cannot break their ranks," said the Swiss, "we have no chance for fight, and our country will be lost!"

Then a poor man, whose name was Ar-nold Wink'el-ried, stepped out.

"On the side of yonder moun-tain," said he, "I have a happy home. There my wife and chil-dren wait for my return. But they will not see me again, for this day I will give my life for my country. And do you, my friends, do your duty, and Switzerland shall be free."

With these words he ran forward. "Follow me!" he cried to his friends. "I will break the lines, and then let every man fight as bravely as he can."

He had nothing in his hands, neither club nor stone nor other weapon. But he ran straight on-ward to the place where the spears were thickest.

"Make way for lib-er-ty!" he cried, as he dashed right into the lines.

A hundred spears were turned to catch him upon their points. The soldiers forgot to stay in their places. The lines were broken. Arnold's friends rushed bravely after him. They fought with whatever they had in hand. They snatched spears and shields from their foes. They had no thought of fear. They only thought of their homes and their dear native land. And they won at last.

Such a battle no one ever knew before. But Switzerland was saved, and Arnold Wink-el-ried did not die in vain.

THE BELL OF ATRI.

A-tri is the name of a little town in It-a-ly. It is a very old town, and is built half-way up the side of a steep hill.

A long time ago, the King of Atri bought a fine large bell, and had it hung up in a tower in the market place. A long rope that reached almost to the ground was fas-tened to the bell. The smallest child could ring the bell by pulling upon this rope.

"It is the bell of justice," said the king.

When at last everything was ready, the people of Atri had a great holiday. All the men and women and children came down to the market place to look at the bell of justice. It was a very pretty bell, and was, pol-ished until it looked almost as bright and yellow as the sun.

"How we should like to hear it ring!" they said.

Then the king came down the street.

"Perhaps he will ring it," said the people; and everybody stood very still, and waited to see what he would do.

But he did not ring the bell. He did not even take the rope in his hands. When he came to the foot of the tower, he stopped, and raised his hand.

"My people," he said, "do you see this beautiful bell? It is your bell; but it must never be rung except in case of need. If any one of you is wronged at any time, he may come and ring the bell; and then the judges shall come together at once, and hear his case, and give him justice. Rich and poor, old and young, all alike may come; but no one must touch the rope unless he knows that he has been wronged."

Many years passed by after this. Many times did the bell in the market place ring out to call the judges together. Many wrongs were righted, many ill-doers were punished. At last the hempen rope was almost worn out. The lower part of it was un-twist-ed; some of the strands were broken; it became so short that only a tall man could reach it.

"This will never do," said the judges one day. "What if a child should be wronged? It could not ring the bell to let us know it."

They gave orders that a new rope should be put upon the bell at once,—a rope that should hang down to the ground, so that the smallest child could reach it. But there was not a rope to be found in all Atri. They would have to send across the mountains for one, and it would be many days before it could be brought. What if some great wrong should be done before it came? How could the judges know about it, if the in-jured one could not reach the old rope?

"Let me fix it for you," said a man who stood by.

He ran into his garden, which was not far away, and soon came back with a long grape-vine in his hands.

"This will do for a rope," he said; and he climbed up, and fastened it to the bell. The slender vine, with its leaves and ten-drils still upon it, trailed to the ground.

"Yes," said the judges, "it is a very good rope. Let it be as it is."

Now, on the hill-side above the village, there lived a man who had once been a brave knight. In his youth he had ridden through many lands, and he had fought in many a battle. His best friend through all that time had been his horse,—a strong, noble steed that had borne him safe through many a danger.

But the knight, when he grew older, cared no more to ride into battle; he cared no more to do brave deeds; he thought of nothing but gold; he became a miser. At last he sold all that he had, except his horse, and went to live in a little hut on the hill-side. Day after day he sat among his money bags, and planned how he might get more gold; and day after day his horse stood in his bare stall, half-starved, and shiv-er-ing with cold.

"What is the use of keeping that lazy steed?" said the miser to himself one morning. "Every week it costs me more to keep him than he is worth. I might sell him; but there is not a man that wants him. I cannot even give him away. I will turn him out to shift for himself, and pick grass by the roadside. If he starves to death, so much the better."

So the brave old horse was turned out to find what he could among the rocks on the barren hill-side. Lame and sick, he strolled along the dusty roads, glad to find a blade of grass or a thistle. The boys threw stones at him, the dogs barked at him, and in all the world there was no one to pity him.

One hot afternoon, when no one was upon the street, the horse chanced to wander into the market place. Not a man nor child was there, for the heat of the sun had driven them all indoors. The gates were wide open; the poor beast could roam where he pleased. He saw the grape-vine rope that hung from the bell of justice. The leaves and tendrils upon it were still fresh and green, for it had not been there long. What a fine dinner they would be for a starving horse!

He stretched his thin neck, and took one of the tempting morsels in his mouth. It was hard to break it from the vine. He pulled at it, and the great bell above him began to ring. All the people in Atri heard it. It seemed to say,—

>"Some one has done me wrong!
>Some one has done me wrong!
>Oh! come and judge my case!
>Oh! come and judge my case!
>For I've been wronged!"

The judges heard it. They put on their robes, and went out through the hot streets to the market place. They wondered who it could be who would ring the bell at such a time. When they passed through the gate, they saw the old horse nibbling at the vine.

"Ha!" cried one, "it is the miser's steed. He has come to call for justice; for his master, as everybody knows, has treated him most shame-ful-ly."

"He pleads his cause as well as any dumb brute can," said another.

"And he shall have justice!" said the third.

Mean-while a crowd of men and women and children had come into the market place, eager to learn what cause the judges were about to try. When they saw the horse, all stood still in wonder. Then every one was ready to tell how they had seen him wan-der-ing on the hills, unfed, un-cared for, while his master sat at home counting his bags of gold.

"Go bring the miser before us," said the judges.

"Some one has done me wrong!"

And when he came, they bade him stand and hear their judg-ment.

"This horse has served you well for many a year," they said. "He has saved you from many a peril. He has helped you gain your wealth.

Therefore we order that one half of all your gold shall be set aside to buy him shelter and food, a green pasture where he may graze, and a warm stall to comfort him in his old age."

The miser hung his head, and grieved to lose his gold; but the people shouted with joy, and the horse was led away to his new stall and a dinner such as he had not had in many a day.

HOW NAPOLEON CROSSED THE ALPS.

About a hundred years ago there lived a great gen-er-al whose name was Na-po´le-on Bo´na-parte. He was the leader of the French army; and France was at war with nearly all the countries around. He wanted very much to take his soldiers into It-a-ly; but between France and Italy there are high mountains called the Alps, the tops of which are covered with snow.

"Is it pos-si-ble to cross the Alps?" said Na-po-le-on.

The men who had been sent to look at the passes over the mountains shook their heads. Then one of them said, "It may be possible, but"—

"Let me hear no more," said Napoleon. "Forward to Italy!"

People laughed at the thought of an army of sixty thousand men crossing the Alps where there was no road. But Napoleon waited only to see that everything was in good order, and then he gave the order to march.

The long line of soldiers and horses and cannon stretched for twenty miles. When they came to a steep place where there seemed to be no way to go farther, the trum-pets sounded "Charge!" Then every man did his best, and the whole army moved right onward.

Soon they were safe over the Alps. In four days they were marching on the plains of Italy.

"The man who has made up his mind to win," said Napoleon, "will never say 'Im-pos-si-ble.'"

THE STORY OF CINCINNATUS.

There was a man named Cin-cin-na´tus who lived on a little farm not far from the city of Rome. He had once been rich, and had held the highest office in the land; but in one way or another he had lost all his wealth. He was now so poor that he had to do all the work on his farm with his own hands. But in those days it was thought to be a noble thing to till the soil.

Cin-cin-na-tus was so wise and just that every-body trusted him, and asked his advice; and when any one was in trouble, and did not know what to do, his neighbors would say,—

"Go and tell Cincinnatus. He will help you."

Now there lived among the mountains, not far away, a tribe of fierce, half-wild men, who were at war with the Roman people. They per-suad-ed another tribe of bold war-riors to help them, and then marched toward the city, plun-der-ing and robbing as they came. They boasted that they would tear down the walls of Rome, and burn the houses, and kill all the men, and make slaves of the women and children.

At first the Romans, who were very proud and brave, did not think there was much danger. Every man in Rome was a soldier, and the army which went out to fight the robbers was the finest in the world. No one staid at home with the women and children and boys but the white-haired "Fathers," as they were called, who made the laws for the city, and a small company of men who guarded the walls. Everybody thought that it would be an easy thing to drive the men of the mountains back to the place where they belonged.

But one morning five horsemen came riding down the road from the mountains. They rode with great speed; and both men and horses were covered with dust and blood. The watchman at the gate knew them, and shouted to them as they gal-loped in. Why did they ride thus? and what had happened to the Roman army?

They did not answer him, but rode into the city and along the quiet streets; and everybody ran after them, eager to find out what was the matter. Rome was not a large city at that time; and soon they reached the market place where the white-haired Fathers were sitting. Then they leaped from their horses, and told their story.

"Only yes-ter-day," they said, "our army was marching through a narrow valley between two steep mountains. All at once a thou-sand sav-age men sprang out from among the rocks before us and above us. They had blocked up the way; and the pass was so narrow that we could not fight. We tried to come back; but they had blocked up the way on this side of us too. The fierce men of the mountains were before us and behind us, and they were throwing rocks down upon us from above. We had been caught in a trap. Then ten of us set spurs to our horses; and five of us forced our way through, but the other five fell before the spears of the mountain men. And now, O Roman Fathers! send help to our army at once, or every man will be slain, and our city will be taken."

"What shall we do?" said the white-haired Fathers. "Whom can we send but the guards and the boys? and who is wise enough to lead them, and thus save Rome?"

All shook their heads and were very grave; for it seemed as if there was no hope. Then one said, "Send for Cincinnatus. He will help us."

Cincinnatus was in the field plowing when the men who had been sent to him came in great haste. He stopped and greeted them kindly, and waited for them to speak.

"Put on your cloak, Cincinnatus," they said, "and hear the words of the Roman people."

Then Cincinnatus wondered what they could mean. "Is all well with Rome?" he asked; and he called to his wife to bring him his cloak.

She brought the cloak; and Cincinnatus wiped the dust from his hands and arms, and threw it over his shoulders. Then the men told their errand.

They told him how the army with all the noblest men of Rome had been en-trapped in the mountain pass. They told him about the great danger the city was in. Then they said, "The people of Rome make you their ruler and the ruler of their city, to do with everything as you choose; and the Fathers bid you come at once and go out against our enemies, the fierce men of the mountains."

So Cincinnatus left his plow standing where it was, and hurried to the city. When he passed through the streets, and gave orders as to what should be done, some of the people were afraid, for they knew that he had all power in Rome to do what he pleased. But he armed the guards and the boys, and went out at their head to fight the fierce mountain men, and free the Roman army from the trap into which it had fallen.

A few days afterward there was great joy in Rome. There was good news from Cincinnatus. The men of the mountains had been beaten with great loss. They had been driven back into their own place.

And now the Roman army, with the boys and the guards, was coming home with banners flying, and shouts of vic-to-ry; and at their head rode Cincinnatus. He had saved Rome.

Cincinnatus might then have made himself king; for his word was law, and no man dared lift a finger against him. But, before the people could thank him enough for what he had done, he gave back the power to the white-haired Roman Fathers, and went again to his little farm and his plow.

He had been the ruler of Rome for sixteen days.

THE STORY OF REGULUS.

On the other side of the sea from Rome there was once a great city named Car-thage. The Roman people were never very friendly to the people of Car-thage, and at last a war began between them. For a long time it was hard to tell which would prove the stronger. First the Romans would gain a battle, and then the men of Car-thage would gain a battle; and so the war went on for many years.

Among the Romans there was a brave gen-er-al named Reg´u-lus,— a man of whom it was said that he never broke his word. It so happened after a while, that Reg-u-lus was taken pris-on-er and carried to Carthage. Ill and very lonely, he dreamed of his wife and little children so far away beyond the sea; and he had but little hope of ever seeing them again. He loved his home dearly, but he believed that his first duty was to his country; and so he had left all, to fight in this cruel war.

He had lost a battle, it is true, and had been taken prisoner. Yet he knew that the Romans were gaining ground, and the people of Carthage were afraid of being beaten in the end. They had sent into other countries to hire soldiers to help them; but even with these they would not be able to fight much longer against Rome.

One day some of the rulers of Carthage came to the prison to talk with Regulus.

"We should like to make peace with the Roman people," they said, "and we are sure, that, if your rulers at home knew how the war is going, they would be glad to make peace with us. We will set you free and let you go home, if you will agree to do as we say."

"What is that?" asked Regulus.

"In the first place," they said, "you must tell the Romans about the battles which you have lost, and you must make it plain to them that they have not gained any-thing by the war. In the second place, you must promise us, that, if they will not make peace, you will come back to your prison."

"Very well," said Regulus, "I promise you, that, if they will not make peace, I will come back to prison."

And so they let him go; for they knew that a great Roman would keep his word.

When he came to Rome, all the people greeted him gladly. His wife and children were very happy, for they thought that now they would not be parted again. The white-haired Fathers who made the laws for the city came to see him. They asked him about the war.

"I was sent from Carthage to ask you to make peace," he said. "But it will not be wise to make peace. True, we have been beaten in a few battles, but our army is gaining ground every day. The people of Carthage are afraid, and well they may be. Keep on with the war a little while longer, and Carthage shall be yours. As for me, I have come to bid my wife and children and Rome fare-well. To-morrow I will start back to Carthage and to prison; for I have promised."

Then the Fathers tried to persuade him to stay.

"Let us send another man in your place," they said.

"Shall a Roman not keep his word?" answered Regulus. "I am ill, and at the best have not long to live. I will go back, as I promised."

His wife and little children wept, and his sons begged him not to leave them again.

"I have given my word," said Regulus. "The rest will be taken care of."

Then he bade them good-by, and went bravely back to the prison and the cruel death which he ex-pect-ed.

This was the kind of courage that made Rome the greatest city in the world.

CORNELIA'S JEWELS.

It was a bright morning in the old city of Rome many hundred years ago. In a vine-covered summer-house in a beautiful garden, two boys were standing. They were looking at their mother and her friend, who were walking among the flowers and trees.

"Did you ever see so handsome a lady as our mother's friend?" asked the younger boy, holding his tall brother's hand. "She looks like a queen."

"Yet she is not so beautiful as our mother," said the elder boy. "She has a fine dress, it is true; but her face is not noble and kind. It is our mother who is like a queen."

"That is true," said the other. "There is no woman in Rome so much like a queen as our own dear mother."

Soon Cor-ne′li-a, their mother, came down the walk to speak with them. She was simply dressed in a plain white robe. Her arms and feet were bare, as was the custom in those days; and no rings nor chains glit-tered about her hands and neck. For her only crown, long braids of soft brown hair were coiled about her head; and a tender smile lit up her noble face as she looked into her sons' proud eyes.

"Boys," she said, "I have something to tell you."

They bowed before her, as Roman lads were taught to do, and said, "What is it, mother?"

"You are to dine with us to-day, here in the garden; and then our friend is going to show us that wonderful casket of jewels of which you have heard so much."

The brothers looked shyly at their mother's friend. Was it possible that she had still other rings besides those on her fingers? Could she have other gems besides those which sparkled in the chains about her neck?

When the simple out-door meal was over, a servant brought the casket from the house. The lady opened it. Ah, how those jewels dazzled the eyes of the wondering boys! There were ropes of pearls, white as milk, and smooth as satin; heaps of shining rubies, red as the glowing coals; sap-phires as blue as the sky that summer day; and di-a-monds that flashed and sparkled like the sunlight.

The brothers looked long at the gems.

"Ah!" whis-pered the younger; "if our mother could only have such beautiful things!"

At last, how-ever, the casket was closed and carried care-ful-ly away.

"Is it true, Cor-ne-li-a, that you have no jewels?" asked her friend. "Is it true, as I have heard it whis-pered, that you are poor?"

"No, I am not poor," answered Cornelia, and as she spoke she drew her two boys to her side; "for here are my jewels. They are worth more than all your gems."

I am sure that the boys never forgot their mother's pride and love and care; and in after years, when they had become great men in Rome, they often thought of this scene in the garden. And the world still likes to hear the story of Cornelia's jewels.

ANDROCLUS AND THE LION.

In Rome there was once a poor slave whose name was An′dro-clus. His master was a cruel man, and so unkind to him that at last An-dro-clus ran away.

He hid himself in a wild wood for many days; but there was no food to be found, and he grew so weak and sick that he thought he should die. So one day he crept into a cave and lay down, and soon he was fast asleep.

After a while a great noise woke him up. A lion had come into the cave, and was roaring loudly. Androclus was very much afraid, for he felt sure that the beast would kill him. Soon, however, he saw that the lion was not angry, but that he limped as though his foot hurt him.

Then Androclus grew so bold that he took hold of the lion's lame paw to see what was the matter. The lion stood quite still, and rubbed his head against the man's shoulder. He seemed to say,—

"I know that you will help me."

Androclus lifted the paw from the ground, and saw that it was a long, sharp thorn which hurt the lion so much. He took the end of the thorn in his fingers; then he gave a strong, quick pull, and out it came. The lion was full of joy. He jumped about like a dog, and licked the hands and feet of his new friend.

Androclus was not at all afraid after this; and when night came, he and the lion lay down and slept side by side.

For a long time, the lion brought food to Androclus every day; and the two became such good friends, that Androclus found his new life a very happy one.

One day some soldiers who were passing through the wood found Androclus in the cave. They knew who he was, and so took him back to Rome.

It was the law at that time that every slave who ran away from his master should be made to fight a hungry lion. So a fierce lion was shut up for a while without food, and a time was set for the fight.

When the day came, thousands of people crowded to see the sport. They went to such places at that time very much as people now-a-days go to see a circus show or a game of base-ball.

The door opened, and poor Androclus was brought in. He was almost dead with fear, for the roars of the lion could al-read-y be heard. He looked up, and saw that there was no pity in the thou-sands of faces around him.

Then the hungry lion rushed in. With a single bound he reached the poor slave. Androclus gave a great cry, not of fear, but of gladness. It was his old friend, the lion of the cave.

The people, who had ex-pect-ed to see the man killed by the lion, were filled with wonder. They saw Androclus put his arms around the lion's neck; they saw the lion lie down at his feet, and lick them lov-ing-ly; they saw the great beast rub his head against the slave's face as though he wanted to be petted. They could not un-der-stand what it all meant.

Androclus and the Lion.

After a while they asked Androclus to tell them about it. So he stood up before them, and, with his arm around the lion's neck, told how he and the beast had lived together in the cave.

"I am a man," he said; "but no man has ever befriended me. This poor lion alone has been kind to me; and we love each other as brothers."

The people were not so bad that they could be cruel to the poor slave now. "Live and be free!" they cried. "Live and be free!"

Others cried, "Let the lion go free too! Give both of them their liberty!"

And so Androclus was set free, and the lion was given to him for his own. And they lived together in Rome for many years.

HORATIUS AT THE BRIDGE.

Once there was a war between the Roman people and the E-trus´cans who lived in the towns on the other side of the Ti-ber River. Por´se-na, the King of the E-trus-cans, raised a great army, and marched toward Rome. The city had never been in so great danger.

The Romans did not have very many fighting men at that time, and they knew that they were not strong enough to meet the Etruscans in open battle. So they kept themselves inside of their walls, and set guards to watch the roads.

One morning the army of Por-se-na was seen coming over the hills from the north. There were thousands of horsemen and footmen, and they were marching straight toward the wooden bridge which spanned the river at Rome.

"What shall we do?" said the white-haired Fathers who made the laws for the Roman people. "If they once gain the bridge, we cannot hinder them from crossing; and then what hope will there be for the town?"

Now, among the guards at the bridge, there was a brave man named Ho-ra´ti-us. He was on the farther side of the river, and when he saw that the Etruscans were so near, he called out to the Romans who were behind him.

"Hew down the bridge with all the speed that you can!" he cried. "I, with the two men who stand by me, will keep the foe at bay."

Then, with their shields before them, and their long spears in their hands, the three brave men stood in the road, and kept back the horsemen whom Porsena had sent to take the bridge.

On the bridge the Romans hewed away at the beams and posts. Their axes rang, the chips flew fast; and soon it trembled, and was ready to fall.

"Come back! come back, and save your lives!" they cried to Ho-ra-ti-us and the two who were with him.

But just then Porsena's horsemen dashed toward them again.

"Run for your lives!" said Horatius to his friends. "I will keep the road."

They turned, and ran back across the bridge. They had hardly reached the other side when there was a crashing of beams and timbers. The bridge toppled over to one side, and then fell with a great splash into the water.

When Horatius heard the sound, he knew that the city was safe. With his face still toward Porsena's men, he moved slowly back-ward till he stood on the river's bank. A dart thrown by one of Porsena's soldiers put out his left eye; but he did not falter. He cast his spear at the fore-most horseman, and then he turned quickly around. He saw the white porch of his own home among the trees on the other side of the stream;

"And he spake to the noble riverThat rolls by the walls of Rome:'O Tiber! father Tiber!To whom the Romans pray,A Roman's life, a Roman's arms,Take thou in charge to-day.'"

He leaped into the deep, swift stream. He still had his heavy armor on; and when he sank out of sight, no one thought that he would ever be seen again. But he was a strong man, and the best swimmer in Rome. The next minute he rose. He was half-way across the river, and safe from the spears and darts which Porsena's soldiers hurled after him.

Soon he reached the farther side, where his friends stood ready to help him. Shout after shout greeted him as he climbed upon the bank. Then Porsena's men shouted also, for they had never seen a man so brave and strong as Horatius. He had kept them out of Rome, but he had done a deed which they could not help but praise.

As for the Romans, they were very grateful to Horatius for having saved their city. They called him Horatius Co´cles, which meant the "one-eyed Horatius," because he had lost an eye in defending the bridge; they caused a fine statue of brass to be made in his honor; and they gave him as much land as he could plow around in a day. And for hundreds of years afterwards—

"With weeping and with laugh-ter,Still was the story told,How well Horatius kept the bridgeIn the brave days of old."

JULIUS CÆSAR.

Nearly two thousand years ago there lived in Rome a man whose name was Julius Cæ´sar. He was the greatest of all the Romans.

Why was he so great?

He was a brave warrior, and had con-quered many countries for Rome. He was wise in planning and in doing. He knew how to make men both love and fear him.

At last he made himself the ruler of Rome. Some said that he wished to become its king. But the Romans at that time did not believe in kings.

Once when Cæ-sar was passing through a little country village, all the men, women, and children of the place came out to see him. There were not more than fifty of them, all together, and they were led by their may-or, who told each one what to do.

These simple people stood by the roadside and watched Cæsar pass. The may-or looked very proud and happy; for was he not the ruler of this village? He felt that he was almost as great a man as Cæsar himself.

Some of the fine of-fi-cers who were with Cæsar laughed. They said, "See how that fellow struts at the head of his little flock!"

"Laugh as you will," said Cæsar, "he has reason to be proud. I would rather be the head man of a village than the second man in Rome!"

At an-oth-er time, Cæsar was crossing a narrow sea in a boat. Before he was halfway to the farther shore, a storm overtook him. The wind blew hard; the waves dashed high; the lightning flashed; the thunder rolled.

It seemed every minute as though the boat would sink. The captain was in great fright. He had crossed the sea many times, but never in such a storm as this. He trembled with fear; he could not guide the boat; he fell down upon his knees; he moaned, "All is lost! all is lost!"

But Cæsar was not afraid. He bade the man get up and take his oars again.

"Why should you be afraid?" he said. "The boat will not be lost; for you have Cæsar on board."

THE SWORD OF DAMOCLES.

There was once a king whose name was Di-o-nys'i-us. He was so unjust and cruel that he won for himself the name of tyrant. He knew that almost everybody hated him, and so he was always in dread lest some one should take his life.

But he was very rich, and he lived in a fine palace where there were many beautiful and costly things, and he was waited upon by a host of servants who were always ready to do his bidding. One day a friend of his, whose name was Dam'o-cles, said to him,—

"How happy you must be! You have here everything that any man could wish."

"Perhaps you would like to change places with me," said the tyrant.

"No, not that, O king!" said Dam-o-cles; "but I think, that, if I could only have your riches and your pleas-ures for one day, I should not want any greater hap-pi-ness."

"Very well," said the tyrant. "You shall have them."

And so, the next day, Damocles was led into the palace, and all the servants were bidden to treat him as their master. He sat down at a table in the banquet hall, and rich foods were placed before him. Nothing was wanting that could give him pleasure. There were costly wines, and beautiful flowers, and rare perfumes, and de-light-ful music. He rested himself among soft cushions, and felt that he was the happiest man in all the world.

The Sword of Damocles.

Then he chanced to raise his eyes toward the ceiling. What was it that was dangling above him, with its point almost touching his head? It was a sharp sword, and it was hung by only a single horse-hair. What if the hair should break? There was danger every moment that it would do so.

The smile faded from the lips of Damocles. His face became ashy pale. His hands trembled. He wanted no more food; he could drink no more wine; he took no more delight in the music. He longed to be out of the palace, and away, he cared not where.

"What is the matter?" said the tyrant.

"That sword! that sword!" cried Damocles. He was so badly frightened that he dared not move.

"Yes," said Di-o-nys-i-us, "I know there is a sword above your head, and that it may fall at any moment. But why should that trouble you? I have a sword over my head all the time. I am every moment in dread lest something may cause me to lose my life."

"Let me go," said Damocles. "I now see that I was mis-tak-en, and that the rich and pow-er-ful are not so happy as they seem. Let me go back to my old home in the poor little cot-tage among the mountains."

And so long as he lived, he never again wanted to be rich, or to change places, even for a moment, with the king.

DAMON AND PYTHIAS.

A young man whose name was Pyth´i-as had done something which the tyrant Dionysius did not like. For this offense he was dragged to prison, and a day was set when he should be put to death. His home was far away, and he wanted very much to see his father and mother and friends before he died.

"Only give me leave to go home and say good-by to those whom I love," he said, "and then I will come back and give up my life."

The tyrant laughed at him.

"How can I know that you will keep your promise?" he said. "You only want to cheat me, and save your-self."

Then a young man whose name was Da-mon spoke and said,—

"O king! put me in prison in place of my friend Pyth-i-as, and let him go to his own country to put his affairs in order, and to bid his friends fare-well. I know that he will come back as he promised, for he is a man who has never broken his word. But if he is not here on the day which you have set, then I will die in his stead."

The tyrant was sur-prised that anybody should make such an offer. He at last agreed to let Pythias go, and gave orders that the young man Da-mon should be shut up in prison.

Time passed, and by and by the day drew near which had been set for Pythias to die; and he had not come back. The tyrant ordered the jailer to keep close watch upon Damon, and not let him escape. But Damon did not try to escape. He still had faith in the truth and honor of his friend. He said, "If Pythias does not come back in time, it will not be his fault. It will be because he is hin-dered against his will."

At last the day came, and then the very hour. Damon was ready to die. His trust in his friend was as firm as ever; and he said that he did not grieve at having to suffer for one whom he loved so much.

Then the jailer came to lead him to his death; but at the same moment Pythias stood in the door. He had been de-layed by storms and ship-wreck, and he had feared that he was too late. He greeted Damon kindly, and then gave himself into the hands of the jailer. He was happy because he thought that he had come in time, even though it was at the last moment.

The tyrant was not so bad but that he could see good in others. He felt that men who loved and trusted each other, as did Damon and Pythias, ought not to suffer un-just-ly. And so he set them both free.

"I would give all my wealth to have one such friend," he said.

A LACONIC ANSWER.

Many miles beyond Rome there was a famous country which we call Greece. The people of Greece were not u-nit-ed like the Romans; but instead there were sev-er-al states, each of which had its own rulers.

Some of the people in the southern part of the country were called Spar-tans, and they were noted for their simple habits and their brav-er-y. The name of their land was La-co'ni-a, and so they were sometimes called La-cons.

One of the strange rules which the Spartans had, was that they should speak briefly, and never use more words than were needed. And so a short answer is often spoken of as being *la-con-ic*; that is, as being such an answer as a Lacon would be likely to give.

There was in the northern part of Greece a land called Mac'e-don; and this land was at one time ruled over by a war-like king named Philip.

Philip of Mac-e-don wanted to become the master of all Greece. So he raised a great army, and made war upon the other states, until nearly all of them were forced to call him their king. Then he sent a letter to the Spartans in La-co-ni-a, and said, "If I go down into your country, I will level your great city to the ground."

In a few days, an answer was brought back to him. When he opened the letter, he found only one word written there.

That word was "IF."

It was as much as to say, "We are not afraid of you so long as the little word 'if' stands in your way."

THE UNGRATEFUL GUEST.

Among the soldiers of King Philip there was a poor man who had done some brave deeds. He had pleased the king in more ways than one, and so the king put a good deal of trust in him.

One day this soldier was on board of a ship at sea when a great storm came up. The winds drove the ship upon the rocks, and it was wrecked. The soldier was cast half-drowned upon the shore; and he would have died there, had it not been for the kind care of a farmer who lived close by.

When the soldier was well enough to go home, he thanked the farmer for what he had done, and promised that he would repay him for his kindness.

But he did not mean to keep his promise. He did not tell King Philip about the man who had saved his life. He only said that there was a fine farm by the seashore, and that he would like very much to have it for his own. Would the king give it to him?

"Who owns the farm now?" asked Philip.

"Only a churlish farmer, who has never done anything for his country," said the soldier.

"Very well, then," said Philip. "You have served me for a long time, and you shall have your wish. Go and take the farm for yourself."

And so the soldier made haste to drive the farmer from his house and home. He took the farm for his own.

The poor farmer was stung to the heart by such treat-ment. He went boldly to the king, and told the whole story from beginning to end. King Philip was very angry when he learned that the man whom he had trusted had done so base a deed. He sent for the soldier in great haste; and when he had come, he caused these words to be burned in his forehead:—

"THE UNGRATEFUL GUEST."

Thus all the world was made to know of the mean act by which the soldier had tried to enrich himself; and from that day until he died all men shunned and hated him.

ALEXANDER AND BUCEPHALUS.

One day King Philip bought a fine horse called Bu-ceph´a-lus. He was a noble an-i-mal, and the king paid a very high price for him. But he was wild and savage, and no man could mount him, or do anything at all with him.

They tried to whip him, but that only made him worse. At last the king bade his servants take him away.

"It is a pity to ruin so fine a horse as that," said Al-ex-an´der, the king's young son. "Those men do not know how to treat him."

"Perhaps you can do better than they," said his father scorn-ful-ly.

"I know," said Al-ex-an-der, "that, if you would only give me leave to try, I could manage this horse better than any one else."

"And if you fail to do so, what then?" asked Philip.

"I will pay you the price of the horse," said the lad.

While everybody was laughing, Alexander ran up to Bu-ceph-a-lus, and turned his head toward the sun. He had noticed that the horse was afraid of his own shadow.

He then spoke gently to the horse, and patted him with his hand. When he had qui-et-ed him a little, he made a quick spring, and leaped upon the horse's back.

Everybody expected to see the boy killed outright. But he kept his place, and let the horse run as fast as he would. By and by, when Bucephalus had become tired, Alexander reined him in, and rode back to the place where his father was standing.

All the men who were there shouted when they saw that the boy had proved himself to be the master of the horse.

He leaped to the ground, and his father ran and kissed him.

"My son," said the king, "Macedon is too small a place for you. You must seek a larger kingdom that will be worthy of you."

After that, Alexander and Bucephalus were the best of friends. They were said to be always together, for when one of them was seen, the other was sure to be not far away. But the horse would never allow any one to mount him but his master.

Alexander became the most famous king and warrior that was ever known; and for that reason he is always called Alexander the Great. Bucephalus carried him through many countries and in many fierce battles, and more than once did he save his master's life.

DIOGENES THE WISE MAN.

At Cor-inth, in Greece, there lived a very wise man whose name was Di-og´e-nes. Men came from all parts of the land to see him and hear him talk.

But wise as he was, he had some very queer ways. He did not believe that any man ought to have more things than he re-al-ly needed; and he said that no man needed much. And so he did not live in a house, but slept in a tub or barrel, which he rolled about from place to place. He spent his days sitting in the sun, and saying wise things to those who were around him.

At noon one day, Di-og-e-nes was seen walking through the streets with a lighted lantern, and looking all around as if in search of something.

"Why do you carry a lantern when the sun is shining?" some one said.

"I am looking for an honest man," answered Diogenes.

When Alexander the Great went to Cor-inth, all the fore-most men in the city came out to see him and to praise him. But Diogenes did not come; and he was the only man for whose o-pin-ions Alexander cared.

Diogenes and Alexander.

And so, since the wise man would not come to see the king, the king went to see the wise man. He found Diogenes in an out-of-the-way place, lying on the ground by his tub. He was en-joy-ing the heat and the light of the sun.

When he saw the king and a great many people coming, he sat up and looked at Alexander. Alexander greeted him and said,—

"Diogenes, I have heard a great deal about your wisdom. Is there anything that I can do for you?"

"Yes," said Diogenes. "You can stand a little on one side, so as not to keep the sunshine from me."

This answer was so dif-fer-ent from what he expected, that the king was much sur-prised. But it did not make him angry; it only made him admire the strange man all the more. When he turned to ride back, he said to his officers,—

"Say what you will; if I were not Alexander, I would like to be Diogenes."

THE BRAVE THREE HUNDRED.

All Greece was in danger. A mighty army, led by the great King of Persia, had come from the east. It was marching along the seashore, and in a few days would be in Greece. The great king had sent mes-sen-gers into every city and state, bidding them give him water and earth in token that the land and the sea were his. But they said,—

"No: we will be free."

And so there was a great stir through-out all the land. The men armed themselves, and made haste to go out and drive back their foe; and the women staid at home, weeping and waiting, and trembling with fear.

There was only one way by which the Per-sian army could go into Greece on that side, and that was by a narrow pass between the mountains and the sea. This pass was guarded by Le-on´i-das, the King of the Spartans, with three hundred Spartan soldiers.

Soon the Persian soldiers were seen coming. There were so many of them that no man could count them. How could a handful of men hope to stand against so great a host?

And yet Le-on-i-das and his Spartans held their ground. They had made up their minds to die at their post. Some one brought them word that there were so many Persians that their arrows dark-ened the sun.

"So much the better," said the Spartans; "we shall fight in the shade."

Bravely they stood in the narrow pass. Bravely they faced their foes. To Spartans there was no such thing as fear. The Persians came forward, only to meet death at the points of their spears.

But one by one the Spartans fell. At last their spears were broken; yet still they stood side by side, fighting to the last. Some fought with swords, some with daggers, and some with only their fists and teeth.

All day long the army of the Persians was kept at bay. But when the sun went down, there was not one Spartan left alive. Where they had stood there was only a heap of the slain, all bristled over with spears and arrows.

Twenty thousand Persian soldiers had fallen before that handful of men. And Greece was saved.

Thousands of years have passed since then; but men still like to tell the story of Leonidas and the brave three hundred who died for their country's sake.

SOCRATES AND HIS HOUSE.

There once lived in Greece a very wise man whose name was Soc′ra-tes. Young men from all parts of the land went to him to learn wisdom from him; and he said so many pleasant things, and said them in so delightful a way, that no one ever grew tired of listening to him.

One summer he built himself a house, but it was so small that his neighbors wondered how he could be content with it.

"What is the reason," said they, "that you, who are so great a man, should build such a little box as this for your dwelling house?"

"Indeed, there may be little reason," said he; "but, small as the place is, I shall think myself happy if I can fill even it with true friends."

THE KING AND HIS HAWK.

Gen′ghis Khan was a great king and war-rior.

He led his army into China and Persia, and he con-quered many lands. In every country, men told about his daring deeds; and they said that since Alexander the Great there had been no king like him.

One morning when he was home from the wars, he rode out into the woods to have a day's sport. Many of his friends were with him. They rode out gayly, carrying their bows and arrows. Behind them came the servants with the hounds.

It was a merry hunting party. The woods rang with their shouts and laughter. They expected to carry much game home in the evening.

On the king's wrist sat his favorite hawk; for in those days hawks were trained to hunt. At a word from their masters they would fly high up into the air, and look around for prey. If they chanced to see a deer or a rabbit, they would swoop down upon it swift as any arrow.

All day long Gen-ghis Khan and his huntsmen rode through the woods. But they did not find as much game as they expected.

Toward evening they started for home. The king had often ridden through the woods, and he knew all the paths. So while the rest of the party took the nearest way, he went by a longer road through a valley between two mountains.

The day had been warm, and the king was very thirsty. His pet hawk had left his wrist and flown away. It would be sure to find its way home.

The king rode slowly along. He had once seen a spring of clear water near this path-way. If he could only find it now! But the hot days of summer had dried up all the moun-tain brooks.

At last, to his joy, he saw some water tric-kling down over the edge of a rock. He knew that there was a spring farther up. In the wet season, a swift stream of water always poured down here; but now it came only one drop at a time.

The king leaped from his horse. He took a little silver cup from his hunting bag. He held it so as to catch the slowly falling drops.

It took a long time to fill the cup; and the king was so thirsty that he could hardly wait. At last it was nearly full. He put the cup to his lips, and was about to drink.

All at once there was a whir-ring sound in the air, and the cup was knocked from his hands. The water was all spilled upon the ground.

The king looked up to see who had done this thing. It was his pet hawk.

The hawk flew back and forth a few times, and then alighted among the rocks by the spring.

The king picked up the cup, and again held it to catch the tric-kling drops.

This time he did not wait so long. When the cup was half full, he lifted it toward his mouth. But before it had touched his lips, the hawk swooped down again, and knocked it from his hands.

And now the king began to grow angry. He tried again; and for the third time the hawk kept him from drinking.

The king was now very angry indeed.

"How do you dare to act so?" he cried. "If I had you in my hands, I would wring your neck!"

Then he filled the cup again. But before he tried to drink, he drew his sword.

"Now, Sir Hawk," he said, "this is the last time."

He had hardly spoken, before the hawk swooped down and knocked the cup from his hand. But the king was looking for this. With a quick sweep of the sword he struck the bird as it passed.

The next moment the poor hawk lay bleeding and dying at its master's feet.

"That is what you get for your pains," said Genghis Khan.

But when he looked for his cup, he found that it had fallen between two rocks, where he could not reach it.

"At any rate, I will have a drink from that spring," he said to himself.

With that he began to climb the steep bank to the place from which the water trickled. It was hard work, and the higher he climbed, the thirst-i-er he became.

At last he reached the place. There indeed was a pool of water; but what was that lying in the pool, and almost filling it? It was a huge, dead snake of the most poi-son-ous kind.

The king stopped. He forgot his thirst. He thought only of the poor dead bird lying on the ground below him.

"The hawk saved my life!" he cried; "and how did I repay him? He was my best friend, and I have killed him."

He clam-bered down the bank. He took the bird up gently, and laid it in his hunting bag. Then he mounted his horse and rode swiftly home. He said to himself,—

"I have learned a sad lesson to-day; and that is, never to do any-thing in anger."

DOCTOR GOLDSMITH.

There was once a kind man whose name was Oliver Gold-smith. He wrote many de-light-ful books, some of which you will read when you are older.

He had a gentle heart. He was always ready to help others and to share with them anything that he had. He gave away so much to the poor that he was always poor himself.

He was some-times called Doctor Goldsmith; for he had studied to be a phy-si-cian.

One day a poor woman asked Doctor Goldsmith to go and see her husband, who was sick and could not eat.

Goldsmith did so. He found that the family was in great need. The man had not had work for a long time. He was not sick, but in distress; and, as for eating, there was no food in the house.

"Call at my room this evening," said Goldsmith to the woman, "and I will give you some med-i-cine for your husband."

In the evening the woman called. Goldsmith gave her a little paper box that was very heavy.

"Here is the med-i-cine," he said. "Use it faith-ful-ly, and I think it will do your husband a great deal of good. But don't open the box until you reach home."

"What are the di-rec-tions for taking it?" asked the woman.

"You will find them inside of the box," he answered.

When the woman reached her home, she sat down by her husband's side, and they opened the box; What do you think they found in it?

It was full of pieces of money. And on the top were the di-rec-tions:—

"TO BE TAKEN AS OFTEN AS NE-CES-SI-TY REQUIRES."

Goldsmith had given them all the ready money that he had.

THE KINGDOMS.

There was once a king of Prussia whose name was Frederick William.

On a fine morning in June he went out alone to walk in the green woods. He was tired of the noise of the city, and he was glad to get away from it.

So, as he walked among the trees, he often stopped to listen to the singing birds, or to look at the wild flowers that grew on every side. Now and then he stooped to pluck a violet, or a primrose, or a yellow but-ter-cup. Soon his hands were full of pretty blossoms.

After a while he came to a little meadow in the midst of the wood. Some children were playing there. They were running here and there, and gathering the cow-slips that were blooming among the grass.

It made the king glad to see the happy children, and hear their merry voices. He stood still for some time, and watched them as they played.

Then he called them around him, and all sat down to-geth-er in the pleasant shade. The children did not know who the strange gentleman was; but they liked his kind face and gentle manners.

"Now, my little folks," said the king, "I want to ask you some ques-tions, and the child who gives the best answer shall have a prize."

Then he held up an orange so that all the children could see.

"You know that we all live in the king-dom of Prussia," he said; "but tell me, to what king-dom does this orange belong?"

The children were puz-zled. They looked at one another, and sat very still for a little while. Then a brave, bright boy spoke up and said,—

"It belongs to the veg-e-ta-ble kingdom, sir."

"Why so, my lad?" asked the king.

"It is the fruit of a plant, and all plants belong to that kingdom," said the boy.

The king was pleased. "You are quite right," he said; "and you shall have the orange for your prize."

He tossed it gayly to the boy. "Catch it if you can!" he said.

Then he took a yellow gold piece from his pocket, and held it up so that it glit-tered in the sunlight.

"Now to what kingdom does this belong?" he asked.

Another bright boy answered quick-ly, "To the min-er-al kingdom, sir! All metals belong to that kingdom."

"That is a good answer," said the king. "The gold piece is your prize."

The children were de-light-ed. With eager faces they waited to hear what the stranger would say next.

"I will ask you only one more question," said the king, "and it is an easy one." Then he stood up, and said, "Tell me, my little folks, to what kingdom do I belong?"

The bright boys were puz-zled now. Some thought of saying, "To the kingdom of Prussia." Some wanted to say, "To the animal kingdom." But they were a little afraid, and all kept still.

At last a tiny blue-eyed child looked up into the king's smiling face, and said in her simple way,—

"I think to the kingdom of heaven."

King Frederick William stooped down and lifted the little maiden in his arms. Tears were in his eyes as he kissed her, and said, "So be it, my child! So be it."

THE BARMECIDE FEAST.

There was once a rich old man who was called the Bar-me-cide. He lived in a beautiful palace in the midst of flowery gardens. He had every-thing that heart could wish.

In the same land there was a poor man whose name was Schac-a-bac. His clothing was rags, and his food was the scraps which other people had thrown away. But he had a light heart, and was as happy as a king.

Once when Schac-a-bac had not had anything to eat for a long time, he thought that he would go and ask the Bar-me-cide to help him.

The servant at the door said, "Come in and talk with our master. He will not send you away hungry."

Schacabac went in, and passed through many beautiful rooms, looking for the Barmecide. At last he came to a grand hall where there were soft carpets on the floor, and fine pictures on the walls, and pleasant couches to lie down upon.

At the upper end of the room he saw a noble man with a long white beard. It was the Barmecide; and poor Schacabac bowed low before him, as was the custom in that country.

The Barmecide spoke very kindly, and asked what was wanted.

Schacabac told him about all his troubles, and said that it was now two days since he had tasted bread.

"Is it possible?" said the Barmecide. "You must be almost dead with hunger; and here I have plenty and to spare!"

Then he turned and called, "Ho, boy! Bring in the water to wash our hands, and then order the cook to hurry the supper."

Schacabac had not expected to be treated so kindly. He began to thank the rich man.

"Say not a word," said the Barmecide, "but let us get ready for the feast."

Then the rich man began to rub his hands as though some one was pouring water on them. "Come and wash with me," he said.

Schacabac saw no boy, nor basin, nor water. But he thought that he ought to do as he was bidden; and so, like the Barmecide, he made a pretense of washing.

"Come now," said the Barmecide, "let us have supper."

He sat down, as if to a table, and pre-tend-ed to be carving a roast. Then he said, "Help yourself, my good friend. You said you were hungry: so, now, don't be afraid of the food."

Schacabac thought that he un-der-stood the joke, and he made pretense of taking food, and passing it to his mouth. Then he began to chew, and said, "You see, sir, I lose no time."

"Boy," said the old man, "bring on the roast goose.—Now, my good friend, try this choice piece from the breast. And here are sweet sauce, honey, raisins, green peas, and dry figs. Help yourself, and remember that other good things are coming."

Schacabac was almost dead with hunger, but he was too polite not to do as he was bidden.

"Come," said the Barmecide, "have another piece of the roast lamb. Did you ever eat anything so de-li-cious?"

"Never in my life," said Schacabac. "Your table is full of good things."

"Then eat heartily," said the Barmecide. "You cannot please me better."

After this came the des-sert. The Barmecide spoke of sweet-meats and fruits; and Schacabac made believe that he was eating them.

"Now is there anything else that you would like?" asked the host.

"Ah, no!" said poor Schacabac. "I have indeed had great plenty."

"Let us drink, then," said the Barmecide. "Boy, bring on the wine!"

"Excuse me, my lord," said Schacabac, "I will drink no wine, for it is for-bid-den."

The Barmecide seized him by the hand. "I have long wished to find a man like you," he said. "But come, now we will sup in earnest."

He clapped his hands. Servants came, and he ordered supper. Soon they sat down to a table loaded with the very dishes of which they had pre-tend-ed to eat.

Poor Schacabac had never had so good a meal in all his life. When they had fin-ished, and the table had been cleared away, the Barmecide said,—

"I have found you to be a man of good un-der-stand-ing. Your wits are quick, and you are ready always to make the best of everything. Come and live with me, and manage my house."

And so Schacabac lived with the Barmecide many years, and never again knew what it was to be hungry.

THE ENDLESS TALE.

In the Far East there was a great king who had no work to do. Every day, and all day long, he sat on soft cush-ions and lis-tened to stories. And no matter what the story was about, he never grew tired of hearing it, even though it was very long.

"There is only one fault that I find with your story," he often said: "it is too short."

All the story-tellers in the world were in-vit-ed to his palace; and some of them told tales that were very long indeed. But the king was always sad when a story was ended.

At last he sent word into every city and town and country place, offering a prize to any one who should tell him an endless tale. He said,—

"To the man that will tell me a story which shall last forever, I will give my fairest daugh-ter for his wife; and I will make him my heir, and he shall be king after me."

But this was not all. He added a very hard con-di-tion. "If any man shall try to tell such a story and then fail, he shall have his head cut off."

The king's daughter was very pretty, and there were many young men in that country who were willing to do anything to win her. But none of them wanted to lose their heads, and so only a few tried for the prize.

One young man invented a story that lasted three months; but at the end of that time, he could think of nothing more. His fate was a warning to others, and it was a long time before another story-teller was so rash as to try the king's patience.

But one day a stran-ger from the South came into the palace.

"Great king," he said, "is it true that you offer a prize to the man who can tell a story that has no end?"

"It is true," said the king.

"And shall this man have your fairest daughter for his wife, and shall he be your heir?"

"Yes, if he suc-ceeds," said the king. "But if he fails, he shall lose his head."

"Very well, then," said the stran-ger. "I have a pleasant story about locusts which I would like to relate."

"Tell it," said the king. "I will listen to you."

The story-teller began his tale.

"Once upon a time a certain king seized upon all the corn in his country, and stored it away in a strong gran-a-ry. But a swarm of locusts came over the land and saw where the grain had been put. After search-ing for many days they found on the east side of the gran-a-ry a crev-ice that was just large enough for one locust to pass through at a time. So one locust went in and carried away a grain of corn; then another locust went in and carried away a grain of corn; then another locust went in and carried away a grain of corn."

Day after day, week after week, the man kept on saying, "Then another locust went in and carried away a grain of corn."

A month passed; a year passed. At the end of two years, the king said,—

"How much longer will the locusts be going in and carrying away corn?"

"O king!" said the story-teller, "they have as yet cleared only one cubit; and there are many thousand cubits in the granary."

"Man, man!" cried the king, "you will drive me mad. I can listen to it no longer. Take my daughter; be my heir; rule my kingdom. But do not let me hear another word about those horrible locusts!"

And so the strange story-teller married the king's daughter. And he lived happily in the land for many years. But his father-in-law, the king, did not care to listen to any more stories.

THE BLIND MEN AND THE ELEPHANT.

There were once six blind men who stood by the road-side every day, and begged from the people who passed. They had often heard of el-e-phants, but they had never seen one; for, being blind, how could they?

It so happened one morning that an el-e-phant was driven down the road where they stood. When they were told that the great beast was before them, they asked the driver to let him stop so that they might see him.

Of course they could not see him with their eyes; but they thought that by touching him they could learn just what kind of animal he was.

The first one happened to put his hand on the elephant's side. "Well, well!" he said, "now I know all about this beast. He is ex-act-ly like a wall."

The second felt only of the elephant's tusk. "My brother," he said, "you are mistaken. He is not at all like a wall. He is round and smooth and sharp. He is more like a spear than anything else."

The third happened to take hold of the elephant's trunk. "Both of you are wrong," he said. "Anybody who knows anything can see that this elephant is like a snake."

The fourth reached out his arms, and grasped one of the elephant's legs. "Oh, how blind you are!" he said. "It is very plain to me that he is round and tall like a tree."

The fifth was a very tall man, and he chanced to take hold of the elephant's ear. "The blind-est man ought to know that this beast is not like any of the things that you name," he said. "He is ex-act-ly like a huge fan."

The sixth was very blind indeed, and it was some time before he could find the elephant at all. At last he seized the animal's tail. "O foolish fellows!" he cried. "You surely have lost your senses. This elephant is not like a wall, or a spear, or a snake, or a tree; neither is he like a fan. But any man with a par-ti-cle of sense can see that he is exactly like a rope."

Then the elephant moved on, and the six blind men sat by the roadside all day, and quar-reled about him. Each believed that he knew just how the animal looked; and each called the others hard names because they did not agree with him. People who have eyes sometimes act as foolishly.

MAXIMILIAN AND THE GOOSE BOY.

One summer day King Max-i-mil´ian of Ba-va´ri-a was walking in the country. The sun shone hot, and he stopped under a tree to rest.

It was very pleasant in the cool shade. The king lay down on the soft grass, and looked up at the white clouds sailing across the sky. Then he took a little book from his pocket and tried to read.

But the king could not keep his mind on his book. Soon his eyes closed, and he was fast asleep.

It was past noon when he awoke. He got up from his grassy bed, and looked around. Then he took his cane in his hand, and started for home.

When he had walked a mile or more, he happened to think of his book. He felt for it in his pocket. It was not there. He had left it under the tree.

The king was already quite tired, and he did not like to walk back so far. But he did not wish to lose the book. What should he do?

If there was only some one to send for it!

While he was thinking, he happened to see a little bare-foot-ed boy in the open field near the road. He was tending a large flock of geese that were picking the short grass, and wading in a shallow brook.

The king went toward the boy. He held a gold piece in his hand.

"My boy," he said, "how would you like to have this piece of money?"

"I would like it," said the boy; "but I never hope to have so much."

"You shall have it if you will run back to the oak tree at the second turning of the road, and fetch me the book that I left there."

The king thought that the boy would be pleased. But not so. He turned away, and said, "I am not so silly as you think."

"What do you mean?" said the king. "Who says that you are silly?"

"Well," said the boy, "you think that I am silly enough to believe that you will give me that gold piece for running a mile, and fetch-ing you a book. You can't catch me."

"But if I give it to you now, perhaps you will believe me," said the king; and he put the gold piece into the little fellow's hand.

The boy's eyes spar-kled; but he did not move.

"What is the matter now?" said the king. "Won't you go?"

The boy said, "I would like to go; but I can't leave the geese. They will stray away, and then I shall be blamed for it."

"Crack the whip!"

"Oh, I will tend them while you are away," said the king.

The boy laughed. "I should like to see you tending them!" he said. "Why, they would run away from you in a minute."

"Only let me try," said the king.

At last the boy gave the king his whip, and started off. He had gone but a little way, when he turned and came back.

"What is the matter now?" said Max-i-mil-ian.

"Crack the whip!"

The king tried to do as he was bidden, but he could not make a sound.

"I thought as much," said the boy. "You don't know how to do anything."

Then he took the whip, and gave the king lessons in whip cracking. "Now you see how it is done," he said, as he handed it back. "If the geese try to run away, crack it loud."

The king laughed. He did his best to learn his lesson; and soon the boy again started off on his errand.

Maximilian sat down on a stone, and laughed at the thought of being a goose-herd. But the geese missed their master at once. With a great cac-kling and hissing they went, half flying, half running, across the meadow.

The king ran after them, but he could not run fast. He tried to crack the whip, but it was of no use. The geese were soon far away. What was worse, they had gotten into a garden, and were feeding on the tender veg-e-ta-bles.

A few minutes after-ward, the goose boy came back with the book.

"Just as I thought," he said. "I have found the book, and you have lost the geese."

"Never mind," said the king, "I will help you get them again."

"Well, then, run around that way, and stand by the brook while I drive them out of the garden."

The king did as he was told. The boy ran forward with his whip, and after a great deal of shouting and scolding, the geese were driven back into the meadow.

"I hope you will pardon me for not being a better goose-herd," said Maximilian; "but, as I am a king, I am not used to such work."

"A king, indeed!" said the boy. "I was very silly to leave the geese with you. But I am not so silly as to believe that you are a king."

"Very well," said Maximilian, with a smile; "here is another gold piece, and now let us be friends."

The boy took the gold, and thanked the giver. He looked up into the king's face and said,—

"You are a very kind man, and I think you might be a good king; but if you were to try all your life, you would never be a good gooseherd."

THE INCHCAPE ROCK.

In the North Sea there is a great rock called the Inch-cape Rock. It is twelve miles from any land, and is covered most of the time with water.

Many boats and ships have been wrecked on that rock; for it is so near the top of the water that no vessel can sail over it without striking it.

More than a hundred years ago there lived not far away a kind-hearted man who was called the Abbot of Ab-er-broth-ock.

"It is a pity," he said, "that so many brave sailors should lose their lives on that hidden rock."

So the abbot caused a buoy to be fastened to the rock. The buoy floated back and forth in the shallow water. A strong chain kept it from floating away.

On the top of the buoy the abbot placed a bell; and when the waves dashed against it, the bell would ring out loud and clear.

Sailors, now, were no longer afraid to cross the sea at that place. When they heard the bell ringing, they knew just where the rock was, and they steered their vessels around it.

"God bless the good Abbot of Ab-er-broth-ock!" they all said.

One calm summer day, a ship with a black flag happened to sail not far from the Inch-cape Rock. The ship belonged to a sea robber called Ralph the Rover; and she was a terror to all honest people both on sea and shore.

There was but little wind that day, and the sea was as smooth as glass. The ship stood almost still; there was hardly a breath of air to fill her sails.

Ralph the Rover was walking on the deck. He looked out upon the glassy sea. He saw the buoy floating above the Inchcape Rock. It looked like a big black speck upon the water. But the bell was not ringing that day. There were no waves to set it in motion.

"Boys!" cried Ralph the Rover; "put out the boat, and row me to the Inchcape Rock. We will play a trick on the old abbot."

The boat was low-ered. Strong arms soon rowed it to the Inchcape Rock. Then the robber, with a heavy ax, broke the chain that held the buoy.

He cut the fas-ten-ings of the bell. It fell into the water. There was a gur-gling sound as it sank out of sight.

"The next one that comes this way will not bless the abbot," said Ralph the Rover.

Soon a breeze sprang up, and the black ship sailed away. The sea robber laughed as he looked back and saw that there was nothing to mark the place of the hidden rock.

For many days, Ralph the Rover scoured the seas, and many were the ships that he plun-dered. At last he chanced to sail back toward the place from which he had started.

The wind had blown hard all day. The waves rolled high. The ship was moving swiftly. But in the evening the wind died away, and a thick fog came on.

Ralph the Rover walked the deck. He could not see where the ship was going. "If the fog would only clear away!" he said.

"I thought I heard the roar of breakers," said the pilot. "We must be near the shore."

"I cannot tell," said Ralph the Rover; "but I think we are not far from the Inchcape Rock. I wish we could hear the good abbot's bell."

The next moment there was a great crash. "It is the Inchcape Rock!" the sailors cried, as the ship gave a lurch to one side, and began to sink.

"Oh, what a wretch am I!" cried Ralph the Rover. "This is what comes of the joke that I played on the good abbot!"

What was it that he heard as the waves rushed over him? Was it the abbot's bell, ringing for him far down at the bottom of the sea?

WHITTINGTON AND HIS CAT.

I. THE CITY.

There was once a little boy whose name was Richard Whit´ting-ton; but everybody called him Dick. His father and mother had died when he was only a babe, and the people who had the care of him were very poor. Dick was not old enough to work, and so he had a hard time of it indeed. Sometimes he had no break-fast, and sometimes he had no dinner; and he was glad at any time to get a crust of bread or a drop of milk.

Now, in the town where Dick lived, the people liked to talk about London. None of them had ever been to the great city, but they seemed to know all about the wonderful things which were to be seen there. They said that all the folks who lived in London were fine gentle-men and ladies; that there was singing and music there all day long; that nobody was ever hungry there, and nobody had to work; and that the streets were all paved with gold.

Dick listened to these stories, and wished that he could go to London.

One day a big wagon drawn by eight horses, all with bells on their heads, drove into the little town. Dick saw the wagon standing by the inn, and he thought that it must be going to the fine city of London.

When the driver came out and was ready to start, the lad ran up and asked him if he might walk by the side of the wagon. The driver asked him some questions; and when he learned how poor Dick was, and that he had neither father nor mother, he told him that he might do as he liked.

It was a long walk for the little lad; but by and by he came to the city of London. He was in such a hurry to see the wonderful sights, that he forgot to thank the driver of the wagon. He ran as fast as he could, from one street to another, trying to find those that were paved with gold. He had once seen a piece of money that was gold, and he knew that it would buy a great, great many things; and now he thought that if he could get only a little bit of the pave-ment, he would have everything that he wanted.

Poor Dick ran till he was so tired that he could run no farther. It was growing dark, and in every street there was only dirt instead of gold. He sat down in a dark corner, and cried himself to sleep.

When he woke up the next morning, he was very hungry; but there was not even a crust of bread for him to eat. He forgot all about the golden pavements, and thought only of food. He walked about from one street to another, and at last grew so hungry that he began to ask those whom he met to give him a penny to buy something to eat.

"Go to work, you idle fellow," said some of them; and the rest passed him by without even looking at him.

"I wish I could go to work!" said Dick.

II. THE KITCHEN.

By and by Dick grew so faint and tired that he could go no farther. He sat down by the door of a fine house, and wished that he was back again in the little town where he was born. The cook-maid, who was just getting dinner, saw him, and called out,—

"What are you doing there, you little beggar? If you don't get away quick, I'll throw a panful of hot dish-water over you. Then I guess you will jump."

Just at that time the master of the house, whose name was Mr. Fitz-war'ren, came home to dinner. When he saw the ragged little fellow at his door, he said,—

"My lad, what are you doing here? I am afraid you are a lazy fellow, and that you want to live without work."

"No, indeed!" said Dick. "I would like to work, if I could find anything to do. But I do not know anybody in this town, and I have not had anything to eat for a long time."

"Poor little fellow!" said Mr. Fitz-war-ren. "Come in, and I will see what I can do for you." And he ordered the cook to give the lad a good dinner, and then to find some light work for him to do.

Little Dick would have been very happy in the new home which he had thus found, if it had not been for the cross cook. She would often say,—

"You are my boy now, and so you must do as I tell you. Look sharp there! Make the fires, carry out the ashes, wash these dishes, sweep the floor, bring in the wood! Oh, what a lazy fellow you are!" And then she would box his ears, or beat him with the broom-stick.

At last, little Alice, his master's daughter, saw how he was treated, and she told the cook she would be turned off if she was not kinder to the lad. After that, Dick had an eas-i-er time of it; but his troubles were not over yet, by any means.

His bed was in a garret at the top of the house, far away from the rooms where the other people slept. There were many holes in the floor and walls, and every night a great number of rats and mice came in. They tor-ment-ed Dick so much, that he did not know what to do.

One day a gentleman gave him a penny for cleaning his shoes, and he made up his mind that he would buy a cat with it. The very next morning he met a girl who was car-ry-ing a cat in her arms.

"I will give you a penny for that cat," he said.

"All right," the girl said. "You may have her, and you will find that she is a good mouser too."

Dick hid his cat in the garret, and every day he carried a part of his dinner to her. It was not long before she had driven all the rats and mice away; and then Dick could sleep soundly every night.

III. THE VENTURE.

Some time after that, a ship that belonged to Mr. Fitzwarren was about to start on a voyage across the sea. It was loaded with goods which were to be sold in lands far away. Mr. Fitzwarren wanted to give his servants a chance for good fortune too, and so he called all of them into the parlor, and asked if they had anything they would like to send out in the ship for trade.

Every one had something to send,—every one but Dick; and as he had neither money nor goods, he staid in the kitchen, and did not come in with the rest. Little Alice guessed why he did not come, and so she said to her papa,—

"Poor Dick ought to have a chance too. Here is some money out of my own purse that you may put in for him."

"No, no, my child!" said Mr. Fitzwarren. "He must risk something of his own." And then he called very loud, "Here, Dick! What are you going to send out on the ship?"

Dick heard him, and came into the room.

"I have nothing in the world," he said, "but a cat which I bought some time ago for a penny."

"Fetch your cat, then, my lad," said Mr. Fitzwarren, "and let her go out. Who knows but that she will bring you some profit?"

Dick, with tears in his eyes, carried poor puss down to the ship, and gave her to the captain. Everybody laughed at his queer venture; but little Alice felt sorry for him, and gave him money to buy another cat.

After that, the cook was worse than before. She made fun of him for sending his cat to sea. "Do you think," she would say, "that puss will sell for enough money to buy a stick to beat you?"

At last Dick could not stand her abuse any longer, and he made up his mind to go back to his old home in the little country town. So, very early in the morning on All-hal-lows Day, he started. He walked as far as the place called Hol-lo-way, and there he sat down on a stone, which to this day is called "Whit-ting-ton's Stone."

As he sat there very sad, and wondering which way he should go, he heard the bells on Bow Church, far away, ringing out a merry chime. He listened. They seemed to say to him,—

"Turn again, Whittington, Thrice Lord Mayor of London."

"Well, well!" he said to himself. "I would put up with almost anything, to be Lord Mayor of London when I am a man, and to ride in a fine coach! I think I will go back and let the old cook cuff and scold as much as she pleases."

Dick did go back, and he was lucky enough to get into the kitchen, and set about his work, before the cook came down-stairs to get break-fast.

IV. THE CAT.

Mr. Fitzwarren's ship made a long voyage, and at last reached a strange land on the other side of the sea. The people had never seen any white men before, and they came in great crowds to buy the fine things with which the ship was loaded. The captain wanted very much to trade with the king of the country; and it was not long before the king sent word for him to come to the palace and see him.

The captain did so. He was shown into a beautiful room, and given a seat on a rich carpet all flow-ered with silver and gold. The king and queen were seated not far away; and soon a number of dishes were brought in for dinner.

They had hardly begun to eat when an army of rats and mice rushed in, and de-voured all the meat before any one could hinder them. The captain wondered at this, and asked if it was not very un-pleas-ant to have so many rats and mice about.

"Oh, yes!" was the answer. "It is indeed un-pleas-ant; and the king would give half his treas-ure if he could get rid of them."

The captain jumped for joy. He remembered the cat which little Whittington had sent out; and he told the king that he had a little creature on board his ship which would make short work of the pests.

Then it was the king's turn to jump for joy; and he jumped so high, that his yellow cap, or turban, dropped off his head.

"Bring the creature to me," he said. "If she will do what you say, I will load your ship with gold."

The captain made believe that he would be very sorry to part with the cat; but at last he went down to the ship to get her, while the king and queen made haste to have another dinner made ready.

The captain, with puss under his arm, reached the palace just in time to see the table crowded with rats. The cat leaped out upon them, and oh! what havoc she did make among the trou-ble-some creatures! Most of them were soon stretched dead upon the floor, while the rest scam-pered away to their holes, and did not dare to come out again.

The king had never been so glad in his life; and the queen asked that the creature which had done such wonders should be brought to her. The captain called, "Pussy, pussy, pussy!" and the cat came up and rubbed against his legs. He picked her up, and offered her to the queen; but at first the queen was afraid to touch her.

However, the captain stroked the cat, and called, "Pussy, pussy, pussy!" and then the queen ventured to touch her. She could only say, "Putty, putty, putty!" for she had not learned to talk English. The captain then put the cat down on the queen's lap, where she purred and purred until she went to sleep.

The king would not have missed getting the cat now for the world. He at once made a bargain with the captain for all the goods on board the ship; and then he gave him ten times as much for the cat as all the rest came to.

The captain was very glad. He bade the king and queen good-by, and the very next day set sail for England.

V. THE FORTUNE.

One morning Mr. Fitzwarren was sitting at his desk in his office. He heard some one tap softly at his door, and he said,—

"Who's there?"

"A friend," was the answer. "I have come to bring you news of your ship 'U-ni-corn.'"

Mr. Fitzwarren jumped up quickly, and opened the door. Whom should he see waiting there but the captain, with a bill of lading in one hand and a box of jewels in the other? He was so full of joy that he lifted up his eyes, and thanked Heaven for sending him such good fortune.

The captain soon told the story of the cat; and then he showed the rich present which the king and queen had sent to poor Dick in payment for her. As soon as the good gentleman heard this, he called out to his servants, —

"Go send him in, and tell him of his fame; Pray call him Mr. Whittington by name."

Some of the men who stood by said that so great a present ought not to be given to a mere boy; but Mr. Fitzwarren frowned upon them.

"It is his own," he said, "and I will not hold back one penny from him."

Dick was scouring the pots when word was brought to him that he should go to the office.

"Oh, I am so dirty!" he said, "and my shoes are full of hob-nails." But he was told to make haste.

Mr. Fitzwarren ordered a chair to be set for him, and then the lad began to think that they were making fun of him.

"I beg that you won't play tricks with a poor boy like me," he said. "Please let me go back to my work."

"Mr. Whittington," said Mr. Fitzwarren, "this is no joke at all. The captain has sold your cat, and has brought you, in return for her, more riches than I have in the whole world."

Then he opened the box of jewels, and showed Dick his treasures.

The poor boy did not know what to do. He begged his master to take a part of it; but Mr. Fitzwarren said, "No, it is all your own; and I feel sure that you will make good use of it."

Dick then offered some of his jewels to his mistress and little Alice. They thanked him, and told him that they felt great joy at his good luck, but wished him to keep his riches for himself.

But he was too kind-heart-ed to keep everything for himself. He gave nice presents to the cap-tain and the sailors, and to the servants in Mr. Fitz-warren's house. He even remembered the cross old cook.

After that, Whittington's face was washed, and his hair curled, and he was dressed in a nice suit of clothes; and then he was as handsome a young man as ever walked the streets of London.

Some time after that, there was a fine wedding at the finest church in London; and Miss Alice became the wife of Mr. Richard Whittington. And the lord mayor was there, and the great judges, and the sher-iffs, and many rich mer-chants; and everybody was very happy.

And Richard Whittington became a great merchant, and was one of the foremost men in London. He was sheriff of the city, and thrice lord mayor; and King Henry V. made him a knight.

He built the famous prison of New-gate in London. On the arch-way in front of the prison was a figure, cut in stone, of Sir Richard

Whittington and his cat; and for three hundred years this figure was shown to all who visited London.

CASABIANCA.

There was a great battle at sea. One could hear nothing but the roar of the big guns. The air was filled with black smoke. The water was strewn with broken masts and pieces of timber which the cannon balls had knocked from the ships. Many men had been killed, and many more had been wounded.

The flag-ship had taken fire. The flames were breaking out from below. The deck was all ablaze. The men who were left alive made haste to launch a small boat. They leaped into it, and rowed swiftly away. Any other place was safer now than on board of that burning ship. There was powder in the hold.

But the captain's son, young Ca-sa-bi-an´ca, still stood upon the deck. The flames were almost all around him now; but he would not stir from his post. His father had bidden him stand there, and he had been taught always to obey. He trusted in his father's word, and be-lieved that when the right time came he would tell him to go.

He saw the men leap into the boat. He heard them call to him to come. He shook his head.

"When father bids me, I will go," he said.

And now the flames were leaping up the masts. The sails were all ablaze. The fire blew hot upon his cheek. It scorched his hair. It was before him, behind him, all around him.

"O father!" he cried, "may I not go now? The men have all left the ship. Is it not time that we too should leave it?"

He did not know that his father was lying in the burning cabin below, that a cannon ball had struck him dead at the very be-gin-ning of the fight. He listened to hear his answer.

"Speak louder, father!" he cried. "I cannot hear what you say."

Above the roaring of the flames, above the crashing of the falling spars, above the booming of the guns, he fancied that his father's voice came faintly to him through the scorching air.

"I am here, father! Speak once again!" he gasped.

But what is that?

A great flash of light fills the air; clouds of smoke shoot quickly upward to the sky; and—

"Boom!"

Oh, what a ter-rif-ic sound! Louder than thunder, louder than the roar of all the guns! The air quivers; the sea itself trembles; the sky is black.

The blazing ship is seen no more.

There was powder in the hold!

A long time ago a lady, whose name was Mrs. Hemans, wrote a poem about this brave boy Ca-sa-bi-an-ca. It is not a very well written poem, and yet everybody has read it, and thousands of people have learned it by heart. I doubt not but that some day you too will read it. It begins in this way:—

"The boy stood on the burning deckWhence all but him had fled;The flame that lit the battle's wreckShone round him o'er the dead.

"Yet beautiful and bright he stood,As born to rule the storm—A creature of heroic blood,A proud though childlike form."

ANTONIO CANOVA.

A good many years ago there lived in Italy a little boy whose name was An-to'ni-o Ca-no'va. He lived with his grand-fa-ther, for his own father was dead. His grand-fa-ther was a stone-cut-ter, and he was very poor.

An-to-ni-o was a puny lad, and not strong enough to work. He did not care to play with the other boys of the town. But he liked to go with his grandfather to the stone-yard. While the old man was busy, cutting and trimming the great blocks of stone, the lad would play among the chips. Sometimes he would make a little statue of soft clay; sometimes he would take hammer and chisel, and try to cut a statue from a piece of rock. He showed so much skill that his grandfather was de-light-ed.

"The boy will be a sculp-tor some day," he said.

Then when they went home in the evening, the grand-moth-er would say, "What have you been doing to-day, my little sculp-tor?"

And she would take him upon her lap and sing to him, or tell him stories that filled his mind with pictures of wonderful and beautiful things. And the next day, when he went back to the stone-yard, he would try to make some of those pictures in stone or clay.

There lived in the same town a rich man who was called the Count. Sometimes the Count would have a grand dinner, and his rich friends from other towns would come to visit him. Then Antonio's grandfather would go up to the Count's house to help with the work in the kitchen; for he was a fine cook as well as a good stone-cut-ter.

It happened one day that Antonio went with his grandfather to the Count's great house. Some people from the city were coming, and there was to be a grand feast. The boy could not cook, and he was not old enough to wait on the table; but he could wash the pans and kettles, and as he was smart and quick, he could help in many other ways.

All went well until it was time to spread the table for dinner. Then there was a crash in the dining room, and a man rushed into the kitchen with some pieces of marble in his hands. He was pale, and trembling with fright.

"What shall I do? What shall I do?" he cried. "I have broken the statue that was to stand at the center of the table. I cannot make the table look pretty without the statue. What will the Count say?"

And now all the other servants were in trouble. Was the dinner to be a failure after all? For everything de-pend-ed on having the table nicely arranged. The Count would be very angry.

"Ah, what shall we do?" they all asked.

Then little Antonio Ca-no-va left his pans and kettles, and went up to the man who had caused the trouble.

"If you had another statue, could you arrange the table?" he asked.

"Cer-tain-ly," said the man; "that is, if the statue were of the right length and height."

"Will you let me try to make one?" asked Anto-nio "Perhaps I can make something that will do."

The man laughed.

"Non-sense!" he cried. "Who are you, that you talk of making statues on an hour's notice?"

"I am Antonio Canova," said the lad.

"Let the boy try what he can do," said the servants, who knew him.

And so, since nothing else could be done, the man allowed him to try.

On the kitchen table there was a large square lump of yellow butter. Two hundred pounds the lump weighed, and it had just come in, fresh and clean, from the dairy on the mountain. With a kitchen knife in his hand, Antonio began to cut and carve this butter. In a few minutes he had molded it into the shape of a crouching lion; and all the servants crowded around to see it.

"How beautiful!" they cried. "It is a great deal pret-ti-er than the statue that was broken."

When it was finished, the man carried it to its place.

"The table will be hand-som-er by half than I ever hoped to make it," he said.

When the Count and his friends came in to dinner, the first thing they saw was the yellow lion.

"What a beautiful work of art!" they cried. "None but a very great artist could ever carve such a figure; and how odd that he should choose to make it of butter!" And then they asked the Count to tell them the name of the artist.

"The servants crowded around to see it."

"Truly, my friends," he said, "this is as much of a surprise to me as to you." And then he called to his head servant, and asked him where he had found so wonderful a statue.

"It was carved only an hour ago by a little boy in the kitchen," said the servant.

This made the Count's friends wonder still more; and the Count bade the servant call the boy into the room.

"My lad," he said, "you have done a piece of work of which the greatest artists would be proud. What is your name, and who is your teacher?"

"My name is Antonio Canova," said the boy, "and I have had no teacher but my grandfather the stonecutter."

By this time all the guests had crowded around Antonio. There were famous artists among them, and they knew that the lad was a genius. They could not say enough in praise of his work; and when at last they sat down at the table, nothing would please them but that Antonio should have a seat with them; and the dinner was made a feast in his honor.

The very next day the Count sent for Antonio to come and live with him. The best artists in the land were em-ployed to teach him the art in which he had shown so much skill; but now, instead of carving butter, he chis-eled marble. In a few years, Antonio Canova became known as one of the greatest sculptors in the world.

PICCIOLA.

Many years ago there was a poor gentleman shut up in one of the great prisons of France. His name was Char-ney, and he was very sad and un-hap-py. He had been put into prison wrong-ful-ly, and it seemed to him as though there was no one in the world who cared for him.

He could not read, for there were no books in the prison. He was not allowed to have pens or paper, and so he could not write. The time dragged slowly by. There was nothing that he could do to make the days seem shorter. His only pastime was walking back and forth in the paved prison yard. There was no work to be done, no one to talk with.

One fine morning in spring, Char-ney was taking his walk in the yard. He was counting the paving stones, as he had done a thousand times before. All at once he stopped. What had made that little mound of earth between two of the stones?

He stooped down to see. A seed of some kind had fallen between the stones. It had sprouted; and now a tiny green leaf was pushing its way up out of the ground. Charney was about to crush it with his foot, when he saw that there was a kind of soft coating over the leaf.

"Ah!" said he. "This coating is to keep it safe. I must not harm it." And he went on with his walk.

The next day he almost stepped upon the plant before he thought of it. He stooped to look at it. There were two leaves now, and the plant was much stronger and greener than it was the day before. He staid by it a long time, looking at all its parts.

Every morning after that, Charney went at once to his little plant. He wanted to see if it had been chilled by the cold, or scorched by the sun. He wanted to see how much it had grown.

One day as he was looking from his window, he saw the jailer go across the yard. The man brushed so close to the little plant, that it seemed as though he would crush it. Charney trembled from head to foot.

"O my Pic-cio-la!" he cried.

When the jailer came to bring his food, he begged the grim fellow to spare his little plant. He expected that the man would laugh at him; but al-though a jailer, he had a kind heart.

"Do you think that I would hurt your little plant?" he said. "No, indeed! It would have been dead long ago, if I had not seen that you thought so much of it."

"That is very good of you, indeed," said Char-ney. He felt half ashamed at having thought the jailer unkind.

Every day he watched Pic-cio-la, as he had named the plant. Every day it grew larger and more beautiful. But once it was almost broken by the huge feet of the jailer's dog. Charney's heart sank within him.

"Picciola must have a house," he said. "I will see if I can make one."

So, though the nights were chilly, he took, day by day, some part of the firewood that was allowed him, and with this he built a little house around the plant.

The plant had a thousand pretty ways which he noticed. He saw how it always bent a little toward the sun; he saw how the flowers folded their petals before a storm.

He had never thought of such things before, and yet he had often seen whole gardens of flowers in bloom.

One day, with soot and water he made some ink; he spread out his hand-ker-chief for paper; he used a sharp-ened stick for a pen—and all for what? He felt that he must write down the doings of his little pet. He spent all his time with the plant.

"See my lord and my lady!" the jailer would say when he saw them.

As the summer passed by, Picciola grew more lovely every day. There were no fewer than thirty blossoms on its stem.

But one sad morning it began to droop. Charney did not know what to do. He gave it water, but still it drooped. The leaves were with-er-ing. The stones of the prison yard would not let the plant live.

Charney knew that there was but one way to save his treasure. Alas! how could he hope that it might be done? The stones must be taken up at once.

But this was a thing which the jailer dared not do. The rules of the prison were strict, and no stone must be moved. Only the highest officers in the land could have such a thing done.

Poor Charney could not sleep. Picciola must die. Already the flowers had with-ered; the leaves would soon fall from the stem.

Then a new thought came to Charney. He would ask the great Napoleon, the em-per-or himself, to save his plant.

It was a hard thing for Charney to do,—to ask a favor of the man whom he hated, the man who had shut him up in this very prison. But for the sake of Picciola he would do it.

He wrote his little story on his hand-ker-chief. Then he gave it into the care of a young girl, who promised to carry it to Napoleon. Ah! if the poor plant would only live a few days longer!

What a long journey that was for the young girl! What a long, dreary waiting it was for Charney and Picciola!

But at last news came to the prison. The stones were to be taken up. Picciola was saved!

The em-per-or's kind wife had heard the story of Charney's care for the plant. She saw the handkerchief on which he had written of its pretty ways.

"Surely," she said, "it can do us no good to keep such a man in prison."

And so, at last, Charney was set free. Of course he was no longer sad and un-lov-ing. He saw how God had cared for him and the little plant, and how kind and true are the hearts of even rough men. And he cher-ished Picciola as a dear, loved friend whom he could never forget.

MIGNON.

Here is the story of Mignon as I remember having read it in a famous old book.

A young man named Wil-helm was staying at an inn in the city. One day as he was going up-stairs he met a little girl coming down. He would have taken her for a boy, if it had not been for the long curls of black hair wound about her head. As she ran by, he caught her in his arms and asked her to whom she belonged. He felt sure that she must be one of the rope-dan-cers who had just come to the inn. She gave him a sharp, dark look, slipped out of his arms, and ran away without speaking.

The next time he saw her, Wil-helm spoke to her again.

"Do not be afraid of me, little one," he said kindly. "What is your name?"

"They call me Mignon," said the child.

"How old are you?" he asked.

"No one has counted," the child an-swered.

Wilhelm went on; but he could not help wondering about the child, and thinking of her dark eyes and strange ways.

One day not long after that, there was a great outcry among the crowd that was watching the rope-dan-cers. Wilhelm went down to find out what was the matter. He saw that the master of the dancers was beating little Mignon with a stick. He ran and held the man by the collar.

"Let the child alone!" he cried. "If you touch her again, one of us shall never leave this spot."

The man tried to get loose; but Wilhelm held him fast. The child crept away, and hid herself in the crowd.

"Pay me what her clothes cost," cried the ropedancer at last, "and you may take her."

As soon as all was quiet, Wilhelm went to look for Mignon; for she now belonged to him. But he could not find her, and it was not until the ropedancers had left the town that she came to him.

"Where have you been?" asked Wilhelm in his kindest tones; but the child did not speak.

"You are to live with me now, and you must be a good child," he said.

"I will try," said Mignon gently.

From that time she tried to do all that she could for Wilhelm and his friends. She would let no one wait on him but herself. She was often seen going to a basin of water to wash from her face the paint with which the ropedancers had red-dened her cheeks: indeed, she nearly rubbed off the skin in trying to wash away its fine brown tint, which she thought was some deep dye.

Mignon grew more lovely every day. She never walked up and down the stairs, but jumped. She would spring along by the railing, and before you knew it, would be sitting quietly above on the landing.

To each one she would speak in a different way. To Wilhelm it was with her arms crossed upon her breast. Often for a whole day she would not say one word, and yet in waiting upon Wilhelm she never tired.

One night he came home very weary and sad. Mignon was waiting for him. She carried the light before him up-stairs. She set the light down upon the table, and in a little while she asked him if she might dance.

"It might ease your heart a little," she said.

Wilhelm, to please her, told her that she might.

Then she brought a little carpet, and spread it upon the floor. At each corner she placed a candle, and on the carpet she put a number of eggs. She arranged the eggs in the form of certain figures. When this was done, she called to a man who was waiting with a violin. She tied a band about her eyes, and then the dancing began.

"And then the dancing began."

How lightly, quickly, nimbly, wonderfully, she moved! She skipped so fast among the eggs, she trod so closely beside them, that you would have thought she must crush them all. But not one of them did she touch. With all kinds of steps she passed among them. Not one of them was moved from its place.

Wilhelm forgot all his cares. He watched every motion of the child. He almost forgot who and where he was.

When the dance was ended, Mignon rolled the eggs together with her foot into a little heap. Not one was left behind, not one was harmed. Then she took the band from her eyes, and made a little bow.

Wilhelm thanked her for showing him a dance that was so wonderful and pretty. He praised her, petted her, and hoped that she had not tired herself too much.

When she had gone from the room, the man with the violin told Wilhelm of the care she had taken to teach him the music of the dance. He told how she had sung it to him over and over again. He told how she had even wished to pay him with her own money for learning to play it for her.

There was yet another way in which Mignon tried to please Wilhelm, and make him forget his cares. She sang to him.

The song which he liked best was one whose words he had never heard before. Its music, too, was strange to him, and yet it pleased him very much. He asked her to speak the words over and over again. He wrote them down; but the sweetness of the tune was more delightful than the words. The song began in this way:—

"Do you know the land where citrons, lemons, grow,
And oranges under the green leaves glow?"

Once, when she had ended the song, she said again, "Do you know the land?"

"It must be Italy," said Wilhelm. "Have you ever been there?"

The child did not answer.

OTHER TALES

JUPITER AND HIS MIGHTY COMPANY.

A long time ago, when the world was much younger than it is now, people told and believed a great many wonderful stories about wonderful things which neither you nor I have ever seen. They often talked about a certain Mighty Being called Jupiter, or Zeus, who was king of the sky and the earth; and they said that he sat most of the time amid the clouds on the top of a very high mountain where he could look down and see everything that was going on in the earth beneath. He liked to ride on the storm-clouds and hurl burning thunderbolts right and left among the trees and rocks; and he was so very, very mighty that when he nodded, the earth quaked, the mountains trembled and smoked, the sky grew black, and the sun hid his face.

Jupiter had two brothers, both of them terrible fellows, but not nearly so great as himself. The name of one of them was Neptune, or Poseidon, and he was the king of the sea. He had a glittering, golden palace far down in the deep sea-caves where the fishes live and the red coral grows; and whenever he was angry the waves would rise mountain high, and the storm-winds would howl fearfully, and the sea would try to break over the land; and men called him the Shaker of the Earth.

The other brother of Jupiter was a sad pale-faced being, whose kingdom was underneath the earth, where the sun never shone and where there was darkness and weeping and sorrow all the time. His name was Pluto, or Aidoneus, and his country was called the Lower World, or the Land of Shadows, or Hades. Men said that whenever any one died, Pluto would send his messenger, or Shadow Leader, to carry that one down into his cheerless kingdom; and for that reason they never spoke well of him, but thought of him only as the enemy of life.

A great number of other Mighty Beings lived with Jupiter amid the clouds on the mountain top,-so many that I can name a very few only.

There was Venus, the queen of love and beauty, who was fairer by far than any woman that you or I have ever seen. There was Athena, or Minerva, the queen of the air, who gave people wisdom and taught them how to do very many useful things. There was Juno, the queen of earth and sky, who sat at the right hand of Jupiter and gave him all kinds of advice. There was Mars, the great warrior, whose delight was in the din of battle. There was Mercury, the swift messenger, who had wings on his cap and shoes, and who flew from place to place like the summer clouds when they are driven before the wind. There was Vulcan, a skillful blacksmith, who had his forge in a burning mountain and wrought many wonderful things of iron and copper and gold. And besides these, there were many others about whom you will learn by and by, and about whom men told strange and beautiful stories.

They lived in glittering, golden mansions, high up among the clouds-so high indeed that the eyes of men could never see them. But they could look down and see what men were doing, and oftentimes they were said to leave their lofty homes and wander unknown across the land or over the sea.

And of all these Mighty Folk, Jupiter was by far the mightiest.

THE GOLDEN AGE.

Jupiter and his Mighty Folk had not always dwelt amid the clouds on the mountain top. In times long past, a wonderful family called Titans had lived there and had ruled over all the world. There were twelve of them-six brothers and six sisters-and they said that their father was the Sky and their mother the Earth. They had the form and looks of men and women, but they were much larger and far more beautiful.

The name of the youngest of these Titans was Saturn; and yet he was so very old that men often called him Father Time. He was the king of the Titans, and so, of course, was the king of all the earth besides.

Men were never so happy as they were during Saturn's reign. It was the true Golden Age then. The springtime lasted all the year. The woods and meadows were always full of blossoms, and the music of singing birds was heard every day and every hour. It was summer and autumn, too, at the same time. Apples and figs and oranges always hung ripe from the trees; and there were purple grapes on the vines, and melons and berries of every kind, which the people had but to pick and eat.

Of course nobody had to do any kind of work in that happy time. There was no such thing as sickness or sorrow or old age. Men and women lived for hundreds and hundreds of years and never became gray or wrinkled or lame, but were always handsome and young. They had no need of houses, for there were no cold days nor storms nor anything to make them afraid.

Nobody was poor, for everybody had the same precious things-the sunlight, the pure air, the wholesome water of the springs, the grass for a carpet, the blue sky for a roof, the fruits and flowers of the woods and meadows. So, of course, no one was richer than another, and there was no money, nor any locks or bolts; for everybody was everybody's friend, and no man wanted to get more of anything than his neighbors had.

When these happy people had lived long enough they fell asleep, and their bodies were seen no more. They flitted away through the air, and over the mountains, and across the sea, to a flowery land in the distant west. And some men say that, even to this day, they are wandering happily hither and thither about the earth, causing babies to smile in their cradles, easing the burdens of the toilworn and sick, and blessing mankind everywhere.

What a pity it is that this Golden Age should have come to an end! But it was Jupiter and his brothers who brought about the sad change.

It is hard to believe it, but men say that Jupiter was the son of the old Titan king, Saturn, and that he was hardly a year old when he began to plot how he might wage war against his father. As soon as he was grown up, he persuaded his brothers, Neptune and Pluto, and his sisters, Juno, Ceres, and Vesta, to join him; and they vowed that they would drive the Titans from the earth.

Then followed a long and terrible war. But Jupiter had many mighty helpers. A company of one-eyed monsters called Cyclopes were kept busy all the time, forging thunderbolts in the fire of burning mountains. Three other monsters, each with a hundred hands, were called in to throw rocks and trees against the stronghold of the Titans; and Jupiter himself hurled his sharp lightning darts so thick and fast that the woods were set on fire and the water in the rivers boiled with the heat.

Of course, good, quiet old Saturn and his brothers and sisters could not hold out always against such foes as these. At the end of ten years they had to give up and beg for peace. They were bound in chains of the hardest rock and thrown into a prison in the Lower Worlds; and the Cyclopes and the hundred-handed monsters were sent there to be their jailers and to keep guard over them forever.

Then men began to grow dissatisfied with their lot. Some wanted to be rich and own all the good things in the world. Some wanted to be kings and rule over the others. Some who were strong wanted to make slaves of those who were weak. Some broke down the fruit trees in the woods, lest others should eat of the fruit. Some, for mere sport, hunted the timid animals which had always been their friends. Some even killed these poor creatures and ate their flesh for food.

At last, instead of everybody being everybody's friend, everybody was everybody's foe.

So, in all the world, instead of peace, there was war; instead of plenty, there was starvation; instead of innocence, there was crime; and instead of happiness, there was misery.

And that was the way in which Jupiter made himself so mighty; and that was the way in which the Golden Age came to an end.

THE STORY OF PROMETHEUS.

I. HOW FIRE WAS GIVEN TO MEN.

In those old, old times, there lived two brothers who were not like other men, nor yet like those Mighty Ones who lived upon the mountain top. They were the sons of one of those Titans who had fought against Jupiter and been sent in chains to the strong prison-house of the Lower World.

The name of the elder of these brothers was Prometheus, or Forethought; for he was always thinking of the future and making things ready for what might happen to-morrow, or next week, or next year, or it may be in a hundred years to come. The younger was called Epimetheus, or Afterthought; for he was always so busy thinking of yesterday, or last year, or a hundred years ago, that he had no care at all for what might come to pass after a while.

For some cause Jupiter had not sent these brothers to prison with the rest of the Titans.

Prometheus did not care to live amid the clouds on the mountain top. He was too busy for that. While the Mighty Folk were spending their time in idleness, drinking nectar and eating ambrosia, he was intent upon plans for making the world wiser and better than it had ever been before.

He went out amongst men to live with them and help them; for his heart was filled with sadness when he found that they were no longer happy as they had been during the golden days when Saturn was king. Ah, how very poor and wretched they were! He found them living in caves and in holes of the earth, shivering with the cold because there was no fire, dying of starvation, hunted by wild beasts and by one another-the most miserable of all living creatures.

"If they only had fire," said Prometheus to himself, "they could at least warm themselves and cook their food; and after a while they could learn to make tools and build themselves houses. Without fire, they are worse off than the beasts."

Then he went boldly to Jupiter and begged him to give fire to men, that so they might have a little comfort through the long, dreary months of winter.

"Not a spark will I give," said Jupiter. "No, indeed! Why, if men had fire they might become strong and wise like ourselves, and after a while they would drive us out of our kingdom. Let them shiver with cold, and let them live like the beasts. It is best for them to be poor and ignorant, that so we Mighty Ones may thrive and be happy."

Prometheus made no answer; but he had set his heart on helping mankind, and he did not give up. He turned away, and left Jupiter and his mighty company forever.

As he was walking by the shore of the sea he found a reed, or, as some say, a tall stalk of fennel, growing; and when he had broken it off he saw that its hollow center was filled with a dry, soft pith which would burn slowly and keep on fire a long time. He took the long stalk in his hands, and started with it towards the dwelling of the sun in the far east.

"Mankind shall have fire in spite of the tyrant who sits on the mountain top," he said.

He reached the place of the sun in the early morning just as the glowing, golden orb was rising from the earth and beginning his daily journey through the sky. He touched the end of the long reed to the flames, and the dry pith caught on fire and burned slowly. Then he turned and hastened back to his own land, carrying with him the precious spark hidden in the hollow center of the plant.

He called some of the shivering men from their caves and built a fire for them, and showed them how to warm themselves by it and how to build other fires from the coals. Soon there was a cheerful blaze in every rude home in the land, and men and women gathered round it and were warm and happy, and thankful to Prometheus for the wonderful gift which he had brought to them from the sun.

It was not long until they learned to cook their food and so to eat like men instead of like beasts. They began at once to leave off their wild and savage habits; and instead of lurking in the dark places of the world, they came out into the open air and the bright sunlight, and were glad because life had been given to them.

After that, Prometheus taught them, little by little, a thousand things. He showed them how to build houses of wood and stone, and how to tame sheep and cattle and make them useful, and how to plow and sow and reap, and how to protect themselves from the storms of winter and the beasts of the woods. Then he showed them how to dig in the earth for copper and iron, and how to melt the ore, and how to hammer it into shape and fashion from it the tools and weapons which they needed in peace and war; and when he saw how happy the world was becoming he cried out:

"A new Golden Age shall come, brighter and better by far than the old!"

II. HOW DISEASES AND CARES CAME AMONG MEN.

Things might have gone on very happily indeed, and the Golden Age might really have come again, had it not been for Jupiter. But one day, when he chanced to look down upon the earth, he saw the fires burning, and the people living in houses, and the flocks feeding on the hills, and the grain ripening in the fields, and this made him very angry.

"Who has done all this?" he asked.

And some one answered, "Prometheus!"

"What! that young Titan!" he cried. "Well, I will punish him in a way that will make him wish I had shut him up in the prison-house with his kinsfolk. But as for those puny men, let them keep their fire. I will make them ten times more miserable than they were before they had it."

Of course it would be easy enough to deal with Prometheus at any time, and so Jupiter was in no great haste about it. He made up his mind to distress mankind first; and he thought of a plan for doing it in a very strange, roundabout way.

In the first place, he ordered his blacksmith Vulcan, whose forge was in the crater of a burning mountain, to take a lump of clay which he gave him, and mold it into the form of a woman. Vulcan did as he was bidden; and when he had finished the image, he carried it up to Jupiter, who was sitting among the clouds with all the Mighty Folk around him. It was nothing but a mere lifeless body, but the great blacksmith had given it a form more perfect than that of any statue that has ever been made.

"Come now!" said Jupiter, "let us all give some goodly gift to this woman;" and he began by giving her life.

Then the others came in their turn, each with a gift for the marvelous creature. One gave her beauty; and another a pleasant voice; and another good manners; and another a kind heart; and another skill in many arts; and, lastly, some one gave her curiosity. Then they called her Pandora, which means the all-gifted, because she had received gifts from them all.

Pandora was so beautiful and so wondrously gifted that no one could help loving her. When the Mighty Folk had admired her for a time, they gave her to Mercury, the light-footed; and he led her down the mountain side to the place where Prometheus and his brother were living and toiling for the good of mankind. He met Epimetheus first, and said to him:

"Epimetheus, here is a beautiful woman, whom Jupiter has sent to you to be your wife."

"Epimetheus, here is a beautiful woman.'"

Prometheus had often warned his brother to beware of any gift that Jupiter might send, for he knew that the mighty tyrant could not be trusted; but when Epimetheus saw Pandora, how lovely and wise she was, he forgot all warnings, and took her home to live with him and be his wife.

Pandora was very happy in her new home; and even Prometheus, when he saw her, was pleased with her loveliness. She had brought with her a golden casket, which Jupiter had given her at parting, and which he had told her held many precious things; but wise Athena, the queen of the air, had warned her never, never to open it, nor look at the things inside.

"They must be jewels," she said to herself; and then she thought of how they would add to her beauty if only she could wear them. "Why did Jupiter give them to me if I should never use them, nor so much as look at them?" she asked.

The more she thought about the golden casket, the more curious she was to see what was in it; and every day she took it down from its shelf and felt of the lid, and tried to peer inside of it without opening it.

"Why should I care for what Athena told me?" she said at last. "She is not beautiful, and jewels would be of no use to her. I think that I will look at them, at any rate. Athena will never know. Nobody else will ever know."

She opened the lid a very little, just to peep inside. All at once there was a whirring, rustling sound, and before she could shut it down again, out flew ten thousand strange creatures with death-like faces and gaunt and dreadful forms, such as nobody in all the world had ever seen. They fluttered for a little while about the room, and then flew away to find dwelling-places wherever there were homes of men. They were diseases and cares; for up to that time mankind had not had any kind of sickness, nor felt any troubles of mind, nor worried about what the morrow might bring forth.

These creatures flew into every house, and, without any one seeing them, nestled down in the bosoms of men and women and children, and put an end to all their joy; and ever since that day they have been flitting and creeping, unseen and unheard, over all the land, bringing pain and sorrow and death into every household.

If Pandora had not shut down the lid so quickly, things would have gone much worse. But she closed it just in time to keep the last of the evil creatures from getting out. The name of this creature was Foreboding, and although he was almost half out of the casket, Pandora pushed him back and shut the lid so tight that he could never escape. If he had gone out into the world, men would have known from childhood just what troubles were going to come to them every day of their lives, and they would never have had any joy or hope so long as they lived.

And this was the way in which Jupiter sought to make mankind more miserable than they had been before Prometheus had befriended them.

III. HOW THE FRIEND OF MEN WAS PUNISHED.

The next thing that Jupiter did was to punish Prometheus for stealing fire from the sun. He bade two of his servants, whose names were Strength and Force, to seize the bold Titan and carry him to the topmost peak of the Caucasus Mountains. Then he sent the blacksmith Vulcan to bind him with iron chains and fetter him to the rocks so that he could not move hand or foot.

Vulcan did not like to do this, for he was a friend of Prometheus, and yet he did not dare to disobey. And so the great friend of men, who had given them fire and lifted them out of their wretchedness and shown them how to live, was chained to the mountain peak; and there he hung, with the storm-winds whistling always around him, and the pitiless hail beating in his face, and fierce eagles shrieking in his ears and tearing his body with their cruel claws. Yet he bore all his sufferings without a groan, and never would he beg for mercy or say that he was sorry for what he had done.

Year after year, and age after age, Prometheus hung there. Now and then old Helios, the driver of the sun car, would look down upon him and smile; now and then flocks of birds would bring him messages from far-off lands; once the ocean nymphs came and sang wonderful songs in his hearing; and oftentimes men looked up to him with pitying eyes, and cried out against the tyrant who had placed him there.

Then, once upon a time, a white cow passed that way,-a strangely beautiful cow, with large sad eyes and a face that seemed almost human. She stopped and looked up at the cold gray peak and the giant body which was chained there. Prometheus saw her and spoke to her kindly:

"I know who you are," he said. "You are Io who was once a fair and happy maiden in distant Argos; and now, because of the tyrant Jupiter and his jealous queen, you are doomed to wander from land to land in that unhuman form. But do not lose hope. Go on to the southward and then to the west; and after many days you shall come to the great river Nile. There you shall again become a maiden, but fairer and more beautiful than before; and you shall become the wife of the king of that land, and shall give birth to a son, from whom shall spring the hero who will break my chains and set me free. As for me, I bide in patience the day which not even Jupiter can hasten or delay. Farewell!"

Poor Io would have spoken, but she could not. Her sorrowful eyes looked once more at the suffering hero on the peak, and then she turned and began her long and tiresome journey to the land of the Nile.

Ages passed, and at last a great hero whose name was Hercules came to the land of the Caucasus. In spite of Jupiter's dread thunderbolts and fearful storms of snow and sleet, he climbed the rugged mountain peak; he slew the fierce eagles that had so long tormented the helpless prisoner on those craggy heights; and with a mighty blow, he broke the fetters of Prometheus and set the grand old hero free.

"I knew that you would come," said Prometheus. "Ten generations ago I spoke of you to Io, who was afterwards the queen of the land of the Nile."

"And Io," said Hercules, "was the mother of the race from which I am sprung."

THE FLOOD.

In those very early times there was a man named Deucalion, and he was the son of Prometheus. He was only a common man and not a Titan like his great father, and yet he was known far and wide for his good deeds and the uprightness of his life. His wife's name was Pyrrha, and she was one of the fairest of the daughters of men.

After Jupiter had bound Prometheus on Mount Caucasus and had sent diseases and cares into the world, men became very, very wicked. They no longer built houses and tended their flocks and lived together in peace; but every man was at war with his neighbor, and there was no law nor safety in all the land. Things were in much worse case now than they had been before Prometheus had come among men, and that was just what Jupiter wanted. But as the world became wickeder and wickeder every day, he began to grow weary of seeing so much bloodshed and of hearing the cries of the oppressed and the poor.

"These men," he said to his mighty company, "are nothing but a source of trouble. When they were good and happy, we felt afraid lest they should become greater than ourselves; and now they are so terribly wicked that we are in worse danger than before. There is only one thing to be done with them, and that is to destroy them every one."

So he sent a great rain-storm upon the earth, and it rained day and night for a long time; and the sea was filled to the brim, and the water ran over the land and covered first the plains and then the forests and then the hills. But men kept on fighting and robbing, even while the rain was pouring down and the sea was coming up over the land.

No one but Deucalion, the son of Prometheus, was ready for such a storm. He had never joined in any of the wrong doings of those around him, and had often told them that unless they left off their evil ways there would be a day of reckoning in the end. Once every year he had gone to the land of the Caucasus to talk with his father, who was hanging chained to the mountain peak.

"The day is coming," said Prometheus, "when Jupiter will send a flood to destroy mankind from the earth. Be sure that you are ready for it, my son."

And so when the rain began to fall, Deucalion drew from its shelter a boat which he had built for just such a time. He called fair Pyrrha, his wife, and the two sat in the boat and were floated safely on the rising waters. Day and night, day and night, I cannot tell how long, the boat drifted hither and thither. The tops of the trees were hidden by the flood, and then the hills and then the mountains; and Deucalion and Pyrrha could see nothing anywhere but water, water, water-and they knew that all the people in the land had been drowned.

After a while the rain stopped falling, and the clouds cleared away, and the blue sky and the golden sun came out overhead. Then the water began to sink very fast and to run off the land towards the sea; and early the very next day the boat was drifted high upon a mountain called Parnassus, and Deucalion and Pyrrha stepped out upon the dry land. After that, it was only a short time until the whole country was laid bare, and the trees shook their leafy branches in the wind, and the fields were carpeted with grass and flowers more beautiful than in the days before the flood.

But Deucalion and Pyrrha were very sad, for they knew that they were the only persons who were left alive in all the land. At last they started to walk down the mountain side towards the plain, wondering what would become of them now, all alone as they were in the wide world. While they were talking and trying to think what they should do, they heard a voice behind them. They turned and saw a noble young prince standing on one of the rocks above them. He was very tall, with blue eyes and yellow hair. There were wings on his shoes and on his cap, and in his hands he bore a staff with golden serpents twined around it. They knew at once that he was Mercury, the swift messenger of the Mighty Ones, and they waited to hear what he would say.

"Is there anything that you wish?" he asked. "Tell me, and you shall have whatever you desire."

"We should like, above all things," said Deucalion, "to see this land full of people once more; for without neighbors and friends, the world is a very lonely place indeed."

"Go on down the mountain," said Mercury, "and as you go, cast the bones of your mother over your shoulders behind you;" and, with these words, he leaped into the air and was seen no more.

"What did he mean?" asked Pyrrha.

"Surely I do not know," said Deucalion. "But let us think a moment. Who is our mother, if it is not the Earth, from whom all living things have sprung? And yet what could he mean by the bones of our mother?"

"As they walked they picked up the loose stones in their way."

"As they walked they picked up the loose stones in their way."

"Perhaps he meant the stones of the earth," said Pyrrha. "Let us go on down the mountain, and as we go, let us pick up the stones in our path and throw them over our shoulders behind us."

"It is rather a silly thing to do," said Deucalion; "and yet there can be no harm in it, and we shall see what will happen."

And so they walked on, down the steep slope of Mount Parnassus, and as they walked they picked up the loose stones in their way and cast them over their shoulders; and strange to say, the stones which Deucalion threw sprang up as full-grown men, strong, and handsome, and brave; and the stones which Pyrrha threw sprang up as full-grown women, lovely and fair. When at last they reached the plain they found themselves at the head of a noble company of human beings, all eager to serve them.

So Deucalion became their king, and he set them in homes, and taught them how to till the ground, and how to do many useful things; and the land was filled with people who were happier and far better than those who had dwelt there before the flood. And they named the country Hellas, after Hellen, the son of Deucalion and Pyrrha; and the people are to this day called Hellenes.

But we call the country GREECE.

THE STORY OF IO.

In the town of Argos there lived a maiden named Io. She was so fair and good that all who knew her loved her, and said that there was no one like her in the whole world. When Jupiter, in his home in the clouds, heard of her, he came down to Argos to see her. She pleased him so much, and was so kind and wise, that he came back the next day and the next and the next; and by and by he stayed in Argos all the time so that he might be near her. She did not know who he was, but thought that he was a prince from some far-off land; for he came in the guise of a young man, and did not look like the great king of earth and sky that he was.

But Juno, the queen who lived with Jupiter and shared his throne in the midst of the clouds, did not love Io at all. When she heard why Jupiter stayed from home so long, she made up her mind to do the fair girl all the harm that she could; and one day she went down to Argos to try what could be done.

Jupiter saw her while she was yet a great way off, and he knew why she had come. So, to save Io from her, he changed the maiden to a white cow. He thought that when Juno had gone back home, it would not be hard to give Io her own form again.

But when the queen saw the cow, she knew that it was Io.

"Oh, what a fine cow you have there!" she said. "Give her to me, good Jupiter, give her to me!"

Jupiter did not like to do this; but she coaxed so hard that at last he gave up, and let her have the cow for her own. He thought that it would not be long till he could get her away from the queen, and change her to a girl once more. But Juno was too wise to trust him. She took the cow by her horns, and led her out of the town.

"Now, my sweet maid," she said, "I will see that you stay in this shape as long as you live."

Then she gave the cow in charge of a strange watchman named Argus, who had, not two eyes only, as you and I have, but ten times ten. And Argus led the cow to a grove, and tied her by a long rope to a tree, where she had to stand and eat grass, and cry, "Moo! moo!" from morn till night; and when the sun had set, and it was dark, she lay down on the cold ground and wept, and cried, "Moo! moo!" till she fell asleep.

But no kind friend heard her, and no one came to help her; for none but Jupiter and Juno knew that the white cow who stood in the grove was Io, whom all the world loved. Day in and day out, Argus, who was all eyes, sat on a hill close by and kept watch; and you could not say that he went to sleep at all, for while half of his eyes were shut, the other half were wide awake, and thus they slept and watched by turns.

Jupiter was grieved when he saw to what a hard life Io had been doomed, and he tried to think of some plan to set her free. One day he called sly Mercury, who had wings on his shoes, and bade him go and lead the cow away from the grove where she was kept. Mercury went down and stood near the foot of the hill where Argus sat, and began to play sweet tunes on his flute. This was just what the strange watchman liked to hear; and so he called to Mercury, and asked him to come up and sit by his side and play still other tunes.

Mercury did as he wished, and played such strains of sweet music as no one in all the world has heard from that day to this. And as he played, queer old Argus lay down upon the grass and listened, and thought that he had not had so great a treat in all his life. But by and by those sweet sounds wrapped him in so strange a spell that all his eyes closed at once, and he fell into a deep sleep.

This was just what Mercury wished. It was not a brave thing to do, and yet he drew a long, sharp knife from his belt and cut off the head of poor Argus while he slept. Then he ran down the hill to loose the cow and lead her to the town.

But Juno had seen him kill her watchman, and she met him on the road. She cried out to him and told him to let the cow go; and her face was so full of wrath that, as soon as he saw her, he turned and fled, and left poor Io to her fate.

Juno was so much grieved when she saw Argus stretched dead in the grass on the hilltop, that she took his hundred eyes and set them in the tail of a peacock; and there you may still see them to this day.

Then she found a great gadfly, as big as a bat, and sent it to buzz in the white cow's ears, and to bite her and sting her so that she could have no rest all day long. Poor Io ran from place to place to get out of its way; but it buzzed and buzzed, and stung and stung, till she was wild with fright and pain, and wished that she were dead. Day after day she ran, now through the thick woods, now in the long grass that grew on the treeless plains, and now by the shore of the sea.

She cried out to him and said "Let the cow go."

By and by she came to a narrow neck of the sea, and, since the land on the other side looked as though she might find rest there, she leaped into the waves and swam across; and that place has been called Bosphorus-a word which means the Sea of the Cow-from that time till now, and you will find it so marked on the maps which you use at school. Then she went on through a strange land on the other side, but, let her do what she would, she could not get rid of the gadfly.

After a time she came to a place where there were high mountains with snow-capped peaks which seemed to touch the sky. There she stopped to rest a while; and she looked up at the calm, cold cliffs above her and wished that she might die where all was so grand and still. But as she looked she saw a giant form stretched upon the rocks midway between earth and sky, and she knew at once that it was Prometheus, the young Titan, whom Jupiter had chained there because he had given fire to men.

"My sufferings are not so great as his," she thought; and her eyes were filled with tears.

Then Prometheus looked down and spoke to her, and his voice was very mild and kind.

"I know who you are," he said; and then he told her not to lose hope, but to go south and then west, and she would by and by find a place in which to rest.

She would have thanked him if she could; but when she tried to speak she could only say, "Moo! moo!"

Then Prometheus went on and told her that the time would come when she should be given her own form again, and that she should live to be the mother of a race of heroes. "As for me," said he, "I bide the time in patience, for I know that one of those heroes will break my chains and set me free. Farewell!"

Then Io, with a brave heart, left the great Titan and journeyed, as he had told her, first south and then west. The gadfly was worse now than before, but she did not fear it half so much, for her heart was full of hope. For a whole year she wandered, and at last she came to the land of Egypt in Africa. She felt so tired now that she could go no farther, and so she lay down near the bank of the great River Nile to rest.

All this time Jupiter might have helped her had he not been so much afraid of Juno. But now it so chanced that when the poor cow lay down by the bank of the Nile, Queen Juno, in her high house in the clouds, also lay down to take a nap. As soon as she was sound asleep, Jupiter like a flash of light sped over the sea to Egypt. He killed the cruel gadfly and threw it into the river. Then he stroked the cow's head with his hand, and the cow was seen no more; but in her place stood the young girl Io, pale and frail, but fair and good as she had been in her old home in the town of Argos. Jupiter said not a word, nor even showed himself to the tired, trembling maiden. He hurried back with all speed to his high home in the clouds, for he feared that Juno might waken and find out what he had done.

The people of Egypt were kind to Io, and gave her a home in their sunny land; and by and by the king of Egypt asked her to be his wife, and made her his queen; and she lived a long and happy life in his marble palace on the bank of the Nile. Ages afterward, the great-grandson of the great-grandson of Io's great-grandson broke the chains of Prometheus and set that mighty friend of mankind free.

The name of the hero was Hercules.

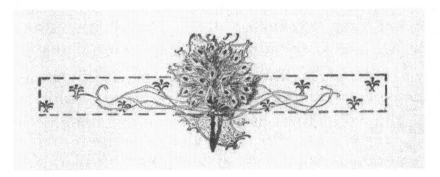

Made in the USA
Middletown, DE
10 August 2024